Amélie Rives

The witness of the sun by Amélie Rives

Amélie Rives

The witness of the sun by Amélie Rives

ISBN/EAN: 9783743367616

Manufactured in Europe, USA, Canada, Australia, Japa

Cover: Foto ©Andreas Hilbeck / pixelio.de

Manufactured and distributed by brebook publishing software (www.brebook.com)

Amélie Rives

The witness of the sun by Amélie Rives

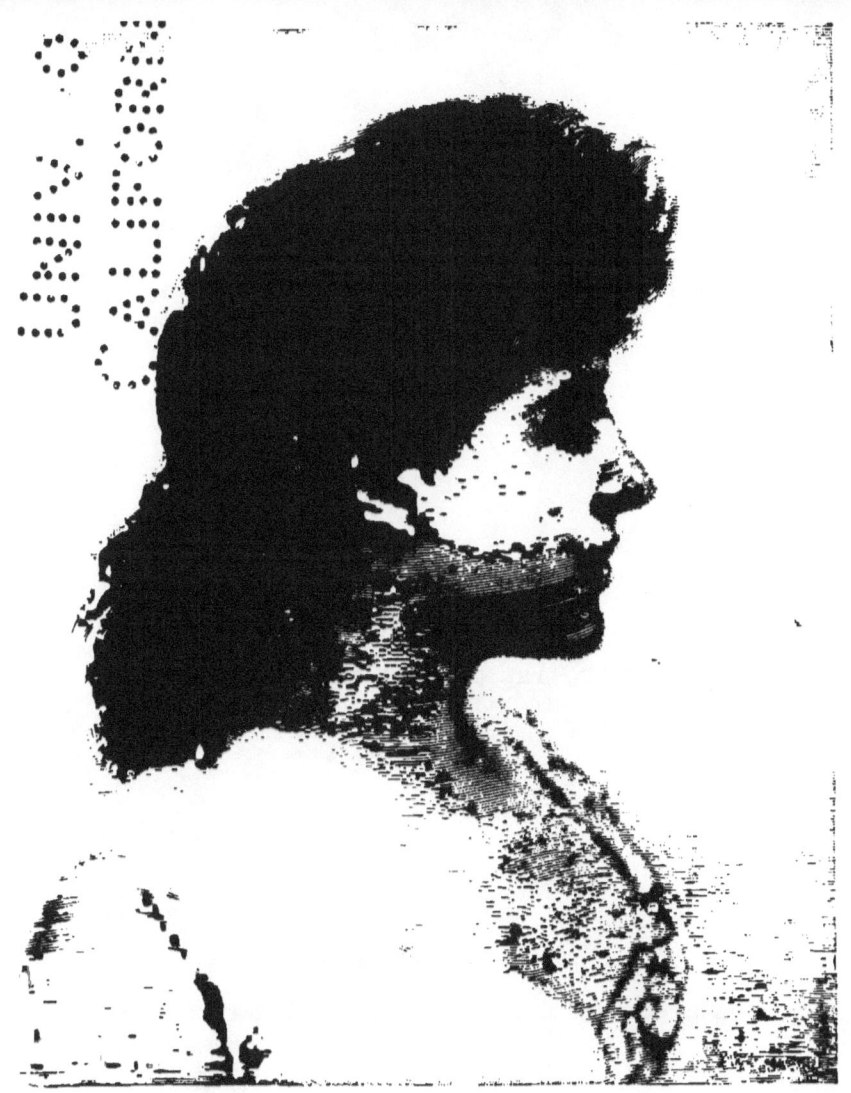

Amélie Rives

THE

WITNESS OF THE SUN.

BY

AMÉLIE RIVES,

AUTHOR OF "THE QUICK OR THE DEAD?" ETC.

"On the earth the broken arcs; in heaven the perfect round."
ROBERT BROWNING.

PHILADELPHIA:
J. B. LIPPINCOTT COMPANY.
1889.

TO

MY DEAR FATHER AND MOTHER,

A THANK-OFFERING.

THE WITNESS OF THE SUN.

I.

WHAT was one to do with a young girl who
sketched ideal heads on her slate underneath half-
finished sums in decimal fractions, who altered the
profiles of the Roman emperors in her Italian history, and who frankly declared that the unexplained
draperies above the figures in the Sistine Madonna
reminded her disagreeably of the parted curtains in a
coupé-lit? Miss Matilda Herbert acknowledged herself at a loss. She even suggested, on occasions, the
advisability of resigning her position as governess in
the Demarini household. To this, however, the
countess would never so much as give ear. Her
good Herbert was as much a part of her daily life
as her warm bath or her mandarin orange before
breakfast. She had superintended the education of
Ilva for ten years, why not for half as many more?
Besides, one could easily prevent any tampering with
the imperial outlines by purchasing an unillustrated
history; and as for the presumptuous criticisms of
Raphael, her good Herbert had only to close her ears
and affect deafness.

When Ilva began the Æneid, however, it was even more painful. She openly ridiculed the famous hero, and not only laughed but drew him to scorn on that ever-to-be-dreaded slate,—yes, pictured him in ghastly white outlines, with tears twice the size of his noble head coursing down entirely to the wooden frame of her slate.

"He is always crying," she said. "*Dio mio!* fancy trying to make a hero of a man who is always as damp as they say the climate of England is! He cries for everything,—absolutely. The fires of love? Pouf! He could have put them out with a bucket of tears in less than twenty minutes. He a hero! He was an ass. See, here are his ears. Look, signorina, I make his ears!" And at this juncture she would hold up the slate with another libellous representation of the celebrated Greek.

Ilva was at ten a very tall child, with a figure which, though delicate, was supple and strong as steel. Her hair, of a pale silverish gold, suggestive of moonlight through amber, grew in five well-defined points above her noble, low brow. Her skin had the clear whiteness of almonds which have been soaked in water. Her eyes, large and lustrous, were the tint of a spring rain-cloud,—that indescribable bluish gray-violet which seems to make blue cold by contrast, gray harsh, and violet sentimental.

Her nose and mouth, while handsome, were too large for her face, at present. In a word, with some very lovely points she was plain, and with decided grace of movement she was, on occasion, awkward. Being entirely aware of these disheartening facts, she felt them the more keenly, perhaps, as her little friend Nathali Zanova was a dainty piece of plump perfection, whose nurse was stopped many times a day with admiring exclamations and inquiries: "Oh, what a beautiful little angel! What hair! What eyes!— like a fawn's. One could see the little beauty was of the nobility;" and then sometimes in an aside, "What a contrast! The other has fine hair and eyes, to be sure, but so pale; and then her mouth and nose! She makes a capital foil, however. The little cherub's mother must be a clever woman." Nathali, for her part, was as conscious of her charms as her friend was of her defects, and had a little strut which she assumed upon the street or in the public gardens, and which irritated Ilva to a limitless degree. This was, of course, when they were much younger. Nathali was now twelve, and Ilva ten.

She was not so intimate with Nathali as of yore, finding her too much occupied in coveting the toilets of her mother's guests, and musing upon the probable magnificence of her future marriage, which she frankly avowed she hoped would take place almost immediately after her *début*. Ilva did not care for toilets, and had startlingly precocious ideas concerning love and matrimony. On the eve of her tenth birthday she had begun a romance in the following manner:

"Married love is like champagne with the sparkles
out." This sentence the good and indefatigable Herbert had found and at once torn up; but, as Ilva
said, with an expressive little grin which showed
both rows of sharp little teeth, "No matter! It is
written in my brain. You cannot tear my brain up
and put it in your waste-basket, Herbert. That is
all."

She was very moderate in her ambitions. She
only desired to become a painter more great than
Sanzio, a poet more original than Dante, and a
novelist more striking than Alessandro Manzoni.

The countess, who was perhaps fonder of her peace
than of the Demarini jewels, did not occupy herself
much with the affairs of her little daughter, beyond
seeing that she had plenty of clothes and school-
books, and taking her sometimes to drive in her
victoria.

Ilva decidedly preferred walking alone to driving
with her mother. At the back of the Villa Demarini there rose abruptly a steep hill, in whose side
were set rough stone steps, which led to a level space
on top, crowned with olive-trees and ilex and the
ruins of a little marble temple. There was also a
marble seat, with some Latin words curving about
its weather-beaten back. There were numberless
grasshoppers and lizards, and a rose-tree which was
in full bloom, its red petals resting upon the broken
limbs of a fallen wood-god below, like drops of

fragrant blood. Still farther up there were pines.
The hill-side was tawny and resinous with the withered needles. The living leaves above seemed ever
mourning their dead comrades below; all night and
all day they sighed ceaselessly. Then there were
always orioles in the great oleanders, so tame that
they would peck crumbs from the girl's hands and
even from the top of her bright head. There could
be nothing more delightful, Ilva thought, than to
lie at one's ease along that old marble seat, with
one's locked hands for a pillow, and watch the restless blue of the sea between the serpent-like stems
of the old olive-trees. Their leaves had the dusty
silver of a moth's wing, even in the brightest sunlight, and their gentle clapper reminded this somewhat fantastic child of a subdued accompaniment of
castanets to which the sunlight danced. One could
see so far, too, on every side. There lay the village
to the right, its white walls and houses glittering in
the garish light, like the foam-cap of that great green
wave of verdure which rolled all the way from the
foot of the distant mountains. Then to the left the
pretty huddling of another little village, farther away,
among its palms and olives and pomegranates and
almond-trees, and the white gleam of the broad road,
and the dashes of color in the skirts of the peasant-
women who moved along it to and from the village,
some with great panniers of lemons and oranges upon
their shoulders, some driving or riding the shag-eared

little donkeys that ambled placidly beneath similar
burdens. ' From this delectable eminence they were
only blurs of pale and ruddy gold to Ilva, in the
same way that the sea was only a vast twinkle, as
vividly blue as the wet wing of a bird that flies
through a sunbeam while one looks.   There were no
waves, only that endless, tireless dance of azure light
which reminded the girl of the breath-broken light
of the sapphires which she was sometimes allowed
to clasp about her mother's throat on grand occasions.
Yes, that was just the way'they shimmered.   How
if one were a giantess and had a giant lover to whom
one might say, " No, never will I be thy wife until
thou hast hardened that sea there into a sapphire
pendant, for which thou must also twist me a great
rope of golden stars and of sunbeams.   Yes, and
when thou hast completed that, I will have thee drag
down the canopy of heaven to make me a robe, and
I will have also the sun for a clasp to my girdle, and
the Milky Way for a veil, and I will have—yes, I
will have—I will have——"

II.

But here she had been interrupted in her soliloquy.
She knew who he was the moment she looked up.
She had seen his photograph the afternoon before,
when she had been allowed to come in for dessert at
luncheon and the people at table had been discussing
him.   He was the young Russian who had just writ-

ten a terrible novel, for which he was to have been
exiled to Siberia, but, owing to some powerful influ-
ence, the Czar had merely banished him instead.
She had wished then with all her heart to see him
and speak with him. She thought perhaps that he
would listen to some of her manuscripts and have a
sympathy for her. She too was going to be a great
novelist. Perhaps she might even be banished from
Italy some day. She had been extremely angry when
her mother told her that she could not possibly allow
her to be at luncheon again to-day. Ilva's anger
was of the steely, white-hot kind that always burns
one's self far more than one's adversary. She had
come to her olive-hidden retreat as usual, and had
brought with her some sheets of note-paper, upon
which she had written again, in large, determined
letters, "Married love is like champagne with the
sparkles out." How that would have impressed the
young Russian,—that sentence which she felt to be
masterly! She was sure no one would have sus-
pected that a little girl of ten had originated it.
And in his photograph he had such kind, deep eyes,
and such a gentle, high-arched mouth. She was
sure that he would have encouraged her and felt for
her. And then to be denied all these delightful possibilities merely because she was yet in short frocks
and wore her hair in a hideous queue! She had
torn the thick bands apart, in a kind of impotent
frenzy, as this thought had come to her, and was

lying back among their riotous splendor, when the voice had interrupted her.

Nadrovine thought her asleep until her murmured soliloquy caught his ear, and he listened in silence until she hesitated; then he interrupted her with these words :

"And what wilt thou have next, little Titaness? Possibly the keys of paradise to hang up in thy drawing-room under a knot of scarlet ribbon. Or is blue thy color?"

"I do not know quite what you mean, signor," she replied, sitting erect, and gathering back her unbound hair with both hands. "I am sorry you heard me saying such silly things. You will think me very foolish."

"I don't see that there was anything very silly in your words," said Nadrovine, kindly. "To tell you the truth, I thought them very pretty. Are all your ideas as big as those?"

"They are not small," she admitted, with some reserve, and a haughtiness which he thought very appropriate to her pale and sternly-cut little features.

"You are one of Madame Demarini's daughters, are you not?" he then asked, following out his own train of thought rather than trying to sustain the thread of their conversation.

She looked at him calmly. "Yes, I am Ilva," she replied. "Please don't mention having found me up here. Nathali's nurse would be sure to think

it a good place for her to play in. Nathali is my
friend,—or used to be."

"You like, then, to be alone?" said Nadrovine, who
was still standing. He chinked some bright pebbles
which he had boyishly transferred from the beach to
his pocket, as he looked down at her gravely. He
thought the pale, unchildish face, with its oriflamme
of vivid hair, singularly interesting and attractive.
"You like to be alone? Is that it?" he repeated.

"Yes, that is it," she answered. "I am never
alone except when I am up here. No one ever
comes here but me, the steps are so steep, and there
is always so much wind. It is not cold, though; it
is never cold here; and if one wants to write, one has
only to make paper-weights of bits of stone. That
statue's three fingers and heel make capital ones, and
the bench is delightful for a table."

"Ah, you write?" said Nadrovine, amused, but
not allowing any sign of it to escape him. He had
known several little girls who wrote, and he was
always very ready indeed to read their manuscripts.
"May I sit there by you?" he said now; "and will
you show me some stories, if you have them up here
with you?"

The swift rush of color to her pale face made her
radiant for a moment. It was as rosy and as sudden
a transformation as that in a pantomime. Nadrovine
saw in that moment that she would probably grow up
to be very beautiful. He was beginning to wonder

what she would read to him from her little blotted
roll of manuscript. They were always blotted, he
remembered, and always in a roll. But, lo! on the
bit of paper she slipped into his hands was only one
sentence, unblotted and heavily legible: "Married
love is like champagne with the sparkles out." He
read it once, once again, and then looked at the little
authoress somewhat curiously.

"What is this, doushka?" he asked. "The title,
or a sentiment that you are going to enlarge upon?
And where did you ever get hold of it?"

Then said Ilva, proudly,—

"It is mine. It is not a title. I wrote it."

"Wrote it? Composed it?" echoed Nadrovine,
looking as astounded as her expectation had pictured
him. Then, with a sudden change of tone, "How
old are you, little one?"

She looked at him, and caught back another wisp
of hair which the wind had blown loose again. "I
am ten,—ten one week ago," she answered. She was
very anxious to know what he would say next, and
moved unconsciously a little nearer to him along the
old marble seat. Then this celebrated and banished
young Russian did a rather strange thing: Ilva,
thinking of it afterwards, wondered how she could
have allowed it. He put a gentle and at the same
time strong arm about her slender shoulders and
drew her to his side, still holding the sheet of paper
in his other hand.

"Doushka," he said, " I have a little cousin whom I love very much. She is just a year older than you. She too wishes to write, and some day I think she will do so to her heart's content. I say to you just what I would say to her, Tear up these words, and try to forget them. Also, never write of what you cannot, in some sort at least, comprehend. Softly, now. Don't be angry with me. Don't pull away. It is a very clever sentence,—cleverer, perhaps, than you have any idea of. It might have been written by one three times your age. Still, it is an unpleasant sort of sentence, too. Let me see. How can I best explain to you? Well, then, for instance, suppose you had said, 'Married love is like champagne, unpalatable and flat when one allows the cork of sympathy to become shrivelled.' That isn't perhaps as clear, but it is more hopeful. If you ever write, doushka,—and I trust you will,—pray, above all things, let your books be hopeful. Do not write so that when one reads one will say, 'Ah, well, in all probability I too will be dragged down into just such a quagmire. What is the use of struggling?' No, make your stories, even those that may be sad, so full of hope that one, having read them, will leap up, saying, 'No matter if things are sad, there is brightness in all. I see no reason why I should not try to be happy like Carlo, or Bettina,' or one of the charming people you are sure to write of. There, that is a neat little sermon, and you furnished the text."

b 2*

Ilva knit her brows, but was not exactly offended. "I do not quite understand why you do not like my sentence, but I hope you do not think it wicked. I only meant it to be true. It seems to me it is like that. I will do as you say, however: I will tear it up." She stripped the sheet of paper, as she spoke, into several little ribbons, and then tore these across once or twice. "There," she ended, slipping them into his hand with a gesture which was both impulsive and imperious. "Keep it to remind you that I promise to do as you say."

"Indeed I will," said the young Russian, heartily. He took the slender, strong little hand and kissed it lightly. "You are to write only what is brave and hopeful," he said, as if speaking to the long fingers which lay upon his palm ; and they tightened slightly in answer.

Then he stooped and lifted a book from the sun-burnt grass. He had at first thought it a pretty box of some sort, for its cover was of old Dutch silver-work, with the Demarini crest set in opals,— altogether a very superb and inappropriate volume to share the siesta of a little girl who wore a rumpled brown holland frock and lay on her back in the sun-shine as regardlessly placid as the lizard that basked near by. He held it on his left hand and opened it. It was a volume of Ariosto's unabridged poems.

"And have you read this, doushka?" he asked, beginning to feel more puzzled and amused and a little horrified. She leaned over and gravely turned one or two leaves with an air of proprietorship.

"Is it not lovely?" she said. "Yes, I have just begun it to-day. I was trying to make some poetry myself when you came."

"And could you not?" said Nadrovine, still smiling rather dubiously.

"No; I do not think I have that talent," she replied, with some sadness. "The rhymes are like so many gnats buz-buz-buzzing, when I only want to fix my ideas. Do you ever write poetry, signor?"

Nadrovine said no, that he did not. Suddenly he put out his hand and drew her down beside him again. "No, I do not write poetry," he repeated. "But I can tell charming fairy-tales. Do you care for fairy-tales?"

"Oh! so much!" exclaimed Ilva.

"Then," said Nadrovine, "I will tell you one. Here it is. There was once a little princess——"

"Do not make it commonplace," interrupted Ilva, with one of her frowns. "I wish you had said a little peasant-girl; all fairy-tales have princesses. But no matter."

Nadrovine laughed, showing teeth which were splendidly white and regular. "My story will disappoint you, I fear," he said, in reply to these rapid interpellations; "but, since my heroine was a princess at first, she must remain one now. She had not a very commonplace name, at all events: they called

her Liott. She also had the most uncommonplace
dwelling conceivable, for she lived in a palace of ice,
which was far more beautiful than anything which
you or I ever saw. She had the most charming
dresses and jewels, and every toy that one can imagine, but her chief delight was in her gardens.
There grew thousands of flowers, from great red
roses like these overhead, to the little wild flowers
that all children love."

"Ah, yes, that is very natural," put in the Signorina Demarini. "I like those much better than
any others myself."

"And I," said Nadrovine, seriously. "One day,
then, Princess Liott was in her garden, which was
separated from the fields beyond by a high hedge,
and, peeping through the hedge, she saw the most
gorgeous blossoms in all the world. She had never
dreamed of such beautiful flowers, not even when
she lay awake at night and pressed her fingers on
her eyelids to see the splendid lilac and gold and
green wreaths that grew and faded and paled and
sparkled again."

"Yes, are they not beautiful?" asked Ilva, becoming absorbed in this not at all commonplace
fairy-tale. "You have so many touches of nature:
that is what makes your books famous, I suppose."

Nadrovine went on without replying:

"The flowers that Princess Liott saw were much
more lovely, and she would have squeezed through

the hedge after them, had not the governess caught
her arm. 'My princess,' said she, 'do not touch
those flowers: they are poisonous, in spite of their
beautiful colors, and will forever stain your little
white hands.' But the princess was haughty and
would not be controlled. She broke from her governess into the lovely field, and gathered the jewel-
like blossoms right and left, until she was tired with
stooping; then she ran back in triumph to show her
governess how silly her warning had been; but later,
when her governess took the great nosegay from
Liott's hands, they were all seamed and blackened,
as though they had been burned, and not only that,
but the fumes had risen from the red and yellow
bells and had blackened poor Princess Liott's fair
skin and dimmed her lovely eyes."

"Was she never pretty again?" said Ilva, slowly.

"She was never quite white again," said Nadrovine; "and she always sat with her hands folded
palms downward in her lap: so I suppose the ugly
stains and seams never went quite away."

"That is a very sad story," said Ilva, still
slowly.

"Doushka," said Nadrovine, "books are sometimes more poisonous than flowers. You see, my
story is commonplace after all: it has a moral."

She kept her bright, direct glance on him, still
turning slowly the leaves of the book which rested
on his knee.

"Is this a bad book?" she said, at last, in a low voice.

"It is not good for you to read, little one."

She suddenly lifted it from his knee. He thought she was going to walk proudly off with her rightful property, but instead she turned with a beautiful, impulsive straightening of both arms towards him.

"Take it," she said. "I give it to you. Keep it, and remember that I have promised you."

Nadrovine was silent a moment, and then drew the child to him.

"This is far too valuable a book for you to give away unpermitted," he said, gently; "but your promise, which is many times more valuable, I take and keep."

She frowned a little, and the gold lights grew in her dark eyes.

"I bid you take it," she said. "It is mine : no one else has a right to it : my grandmother left it to me in her will when I was—oh ! a mere speck—a baby. Here; that is my name. You see? Take it."

Nadrovine was extremely touched.

"Doushka," he said, and as he spoke he put a shapely brown hand on her blowing hair, "I cannot take your beautiful book for my very own, but I will keep it gladly until you wish for it again."

She said nothing in answer, and, stooping towards her, he saw that her eyes were full of tears.

"You are very good to me," she said, in a stifled

voice. "You seem to care. Why do you? No one else does. I might read every book in the house if I chose. Nathali is watched over and cared for. She is so beautiful. Have you seen her? But I— I am ugly!"

And she turned and rushed away from him down the rough, irregular steps, sobbing as she went, and leaving a very perplexed and astounded young Russian novelist behind her.

She did not see him again until she was seventeen.

III.

This little episode with Nadrovine had a distinct effect upon the girl's character. There were many things every day that she denied herself, in thinking that he would not have approved them. She seemed to herself to have become the Princess Liott of his little allegory, and was very bent on keeping her hands clean at least, since they could not be small and white like Nathali's. She no longer drove the dusty toads from under the big aloes, into the little pool on the east terrace. She tried not to say insolent things to the very exasperating Herbert. She bore like a Stoic such lies as Nathali saw fit to tell of her from time to time, and she abandoned her alterations in the profiles of the Roman emperors, in order that she might give her undivided attention to the reproduction of Nadrovine's sharply-cut features. He became to her a sort of embodied conscience, and

she fell into one of those pure and romantic idola-
tries of which only an innocent girl is capable. She
heard of him very often. Sometimes her father and
mother would discuss his career and personality.
Sometimes the guests at the villa would do so.
Sometimes she would herself see articles in the different papers concerning him. He was founder of
a new school, they said, one which did not pluck
the wings from ideals and leave them to crawl, but
which pointed out a possible butterfly in every ugly,
realistic grub which nibbled the flowers of rhetoric.
The child carefully cut out such articles and put
them away in a little enamelled box which had once
held bon-bons. This box had a lock and key, and
she wore the key about her throat on a bit of ribbon.
As his profile dominated all her sketches, so what
she fancied to be his character was given to every
hero in her fantastic stories. As the years went by,
however, his wraith became paler and more transparent, until, instead of coloring circumstances, as it
were, the vivid hues of surrounding facts became
more and more apparent through its dwindling mist.

When Ilva was seventeen, she told herself that she
had been ridiculously sentimental, and that this Nadrovine whom she had adored so long would be the
first to smile at her for a romantic little school-girl.
She still kept the newspaper cuttings which spoke of
him, however, but she took the key from about her
neck and put it in her writing-desk.

She often thought of the hour when she and Na-drovine would meet again, and whether he had kept the silver book, as he had promised, all these years. She wondered, in fact, if he remembered her.

One day the countess said, as they sat together on the terrace late in the afternoon,—

"By the way, Ilva, Nadrovine, the great writer, comes here this evening to dine. Your father brings him. It is only a family dinner; and, as there is such an awkward number, I am going to permit you to dine with us."

"I shall like it very much. You are very kind, mamma," said the girl. Her heart beat a good deal, and she felt that the color had risen to her cheeks. It was so strange to think that she was to see him after all these years, and so very pleasant to think how different he would find her, in appearance at least, from what she had been at their last interview.

She was very careful with her toilet that evening, plaiting and replaiting, herself, the luxurious swaths of her hair, until they were as lustrous as so many twisted flames, pinning the knot of tea-roses which she was to wear in five different places on her corsage, and stopping at the last moment while her maid sewed new rosettes on a pair of bronze shoes which she particularly fancied.

"Ah," said Nadrovine to himself, when she entered the room, "she is as lovely as I thought she would be."

Her childishly simple gown of white gauze was
cut squarely from her long and supple throat, and
fawn-colored gloves came up nearly to the puffed
sleeves which surmounted her graceful shoulders
like some airy order of epaulets. There was a
gold-colored ribbon about her waist, and a knot of
it among the lace at her breast. The tea-roses
were mingled with the lace and ribbon.

As for Nadrovine, he had not changed in the least.
He was now twenty-nine, but his light-brown curls
were as free from any tinge of gray as they had been
seven years ago, and he carried himself with as virile
a grace. When he smiled on speaking to her for the
first time, she saw that his teeth were as brilliantly
regular as ever and his mouth as handsome. He had
the thin curled lips which, when not cruel, are so
beautiful. Ilva thought of numberless things which
she would like to say to him. She wondered, should
they chance to be thrown together for a few moments,
what he would first say to her. After dinner they
went out on the terrace and had cigarettes and coffee
and liqueurs. There was much soft moonlight
through a silver fleece of clouds. It made transparent the tender leaves of a young grape-vine
near which the girl sat, and threw delicate moving
shadows over her white gown and arms. She had
wound some thin white stuff about her head and
shoulders, and the golden ribbons at her waist and
bosom reminded him of stray sunbeams. Some peo-

ple had just called informally, and he came and sat down· in a great bamboo chair near her, while they were making their greetings.

"You have never asked for the silver book," was what he said to her; and she replied, not lightly as she had meant to, but very seriously,—

"And I never will."

"What! you will never read Ariosto?" said Nadrovine, smiling. "I find him a charming poet."

This was not quite what Ilva had expected. She returned his smile with a rather haughty look.

"I dare say I should find him charming also," she replied, after perhaps a second's pause. "It is merely a whim."

"So, then, you have whims, like any other mortal, signorina?" said Nadrovine, still smiling. "I fancied that you were going to develop into a startlingly original young lady, from the glimpse I had of your childhood. I have whims myself. They are very disagreeable. Take my advice, and give them to me to keep with the silver book."

Ilva thought him impertinent. She was bitterly disappointed. Her pretty, childish breast swelled angrily under its knot of gold ribbons. Is anything· so annoying to a young girl as to be taken for exactly the age that she is? She was just seventeen, and he treated her as he would have done any other little girl of seventeen. She began to dislike him. She began to find disagreeable the lines of that sharp-cut profile which she had so often drawn on slate and paper and even on the stiff hem of her white petticoats.   He was apparently absorbed in his own thoughts during the silence which followed. He leaned his head back against the olive-wood trellis that supported the grape-vine, and allowed the smoke of his cigarette to escape through his handsome nostrils.   He was, in fact, thinking of her,—gentle and tender thoughts, such as some men will give young girls into whose pure minds they see as through a crystal opening.   He thought her renunciation of Ariosto as lovely as it was childish, and, seeing that she was offended, regretted having teased her.   He turned suddenly and threw away his cigarette.

"Doushka," he said,—how well she remembered the tone of his voice as he pronounced the odd little Russian word!—"see, do not be angry with me.   It was only in jest that I spoke.   It is very good and lovely of you to have kept your promise all these years.   I am going to ask you to let me send you back your silver book with marks at those passages which I think you would enjoy.   Will you?"

The feeling of personal dislike for him melted away with these words, but the annoyance at being addressed as though she were a child increased, if possible.

"You are very good," she said, a trifle stiffly.

"Ah, you said that to me once before," replied

Nadrovine, with the smile which she was beginning to watch for, "but so differently. There were tears in your voice as well as in your eyes then. What a strange little creature you were!" he went on, speaking more to himself than to her. "I have often regretted that I did not see more of you as a child."

"Perhaps you would have had more regrets the more you saw of me," said the girl, slowly. "I believe that I was a very disagreeable child."

Nadrovine made a light gesture of dissent. "Oh, we should have understood each other," he said, easily.

"Do you think so?" asked Ilva. She held a little fan of amber with gold ribbons between her eyes and the moonlit glare of the sea. He thought that the moonlight shining through it reproduced the tint of her hair exactly. She could not make out his expression, for the background of sparkling water. Nadrovine caught the nettled tone in her voice.

"Why? Do you think so?" he said, gently.

"Oh! I? How can I tell?" she answered, arranging her roses. "It is your gift to guess at situations. You are famous for it. If you say so, yes, I suppose we should have understood each other, —yes, assuredly."

"You mean that we do not understand each other now," said Nadrovine. She replied by another question.

"Do you think we do?" she said; but, before he could answer, the countess approached with some guests who wished to meet Nadrovine, and Ilva spoke no more alone with him that evening.

She went to her room feeling a good deal as though she had lifted a charming flower to her face and the bee within had stung her. She had thought so often of this meeting, had listened so many times to the earnest, beautiful things he would probably say to her. She had even committed one of her prettiest poems to memory in order that she might repeat it to him when he inquired about her writings. She remembered with a fresh feeling of irritated disappointment that he had not asked so much as one question concerning them. Altogether, it had been a very flat and uneventful conversation. He had only said what any other man might have said under the circumstances, and she, on her side, had only been rather rude, she was afraid.

Nathali Zanova came over the next morning full of the celebrated Russian's advent in the neighborhood.

"And you actually sat at the same table with him!" said she. "*Dio mio!* that I had been inspired to ask myself to dine yesterday! What did he talk of? They say he is as beautiful as a Greek god. Is he?"

"Some Greek gods are very ugly; don't you think so?" said Ilva, chillily. "There is one in the

Vatican with a broken nose who is quite hideous. Signor Nadrovine is not at all like him. I don't think he is like any of them."

" Ebbene, I should have said like one's dream of a Greek god," cried Nathali. "You dear, literal girl !" She took Ilva about the waist and attempted to kiss her.

" Please do not, Nathali," said the girl. "You know I do not like to be kissed."

" Yes, by me," said Nathali, good-humoredly ; "and yet I have very pretty lips. Ebbene, wait until you have a lover."

" I shall never kiss any man but my husband," Ilva replied, with loftiness.

" Oh-h ! so there is going to be a husband, then, after all," said Signorina Zanova, smiling her large-toothed but still pretty smile. "A month ago you were never going to marry."

" One can never tell," answered Ilva, calmly, notwithstanding, however, she blushed rather warmly. Nathali was almost as exasperating on occasions as the good Herbert. She was a very large-limbed woman, not so tall as Ilva, with a pale, well-cut, rather voluptuous mouth, which was generally open in a perpetual air of wonder, eyes which were too wide apart, and coarse, beautifully brown hair, cut abundantly above her thick eyebrows. Her figure, although well shaped, was too compact to be graceful. One always felt that it must be with a sense of duty accomplished that the Signorina Zanova unbuttoned her corsage at night. She was a woman who became herself extremely, if one may be allowed a certain liberty of expression,—that is, her mind harmonized entirely with her physique. Had she been allowed to select a body to contain her soul, one felt quite certain that her present shape would have been her choice. Her big limbs ended in the tiny hands and feet which are the ideal of beauty with so many women and which men generally fail to admire. As a little girl, Nathali had possessed the arms of a well-stuffed chair and the legs of a piano. As a young lady, voluminous sleeves and draperies only permitted one to observe hands which corresponded to the little tassels which usually finish off chair-arms and feet not much larger than the casters in which piano-legs always terminate. She was nineteen, and had been in society for a year, and was always consciously or unconsciously reminding Ilva of her less fortunate position. She would rush over to the Villa Demarini, on the day after a ball, with handfuls of gay ribbons which she had received in the cotillon and which she ostensibly brought for the collars of Ilva's dogs. Ilva, for her part, was quite sure that Nathali really brought them to show what a success she had had at the ball. Nathali's purse was as well filled as her bodice, which may perhaps somewhat account for the brilliancy of her social career, and she had an American friend, a woman

even larger and more exuberant of limb than herself, who taught her to emulate the little Joseph in
apparel and to use American slang. This being
sometimes translated into Italian was a very astound-
ing thing to hear.

The difference in the feelings of the two girls for
each other may perhaps be concisely explained by
saying that the ways of Ilva wearied Nathali, while
Nathali herself wearied Ilva. She would often escape,
when she saw the Zanova coupé approaching, and run
far out into the great orange-gardens that flanked the
house. Sometimes it would be her fate to be inter-
cepted in her flight. To-day was one of those days;
and, to complete matters, Nathali insisted upon talking of Nadrovine.

"My dearest child," she now proceeded to remark,
"do you know they say that, although he is so distinguished, he is a perfect Don Juan?"

"I forbid you to say any more," interrupted Ilva,
in a tensely quiet voice. Her eyes had those golden
lights which flash in the eyes of some angry dogs,
and which with her always meant violent emotion of
some sort. She went and threw wide the venetian
blinds of one of her windows. "Is it that Mees
Sherlow who has taught you such conversation?"
she continued, leaning against the window, and not
regarding Nathali, whose mouth was more open than
usual. "If it is so, do not think that I will listen
to it. Such talk is abominable, disgusting, odious

c

to me. You used not to say such things, Nathali.
It is like the fairy-tale where the toads fell out of
the girl's mouth. You might as well come and
pour a handful of mud into my lap: I would thank
you quite as much."

Nathali turned quite pale.

"You are horridly rude," she said. She took off
her heavy rings and tossed them in her two hands
with an attempt at carelessness. "There is nothing
so odious as a prude," she remarked, after a while.

"Except a woman who repeats unclean stories and
anecdotes," replied Ilva, coolly.

"I do not repeat unclean anecdotes," said Nathali,
sullenly. She rose and put on her rings again, and
took up her sunshade, which bristled with orange-
and cherry-colored ribbons. "It is nothing to say
that a man is a Don Juan. All men sow their wild
oats nowadays. If Nadrovine were not a——"

"Do not dare to say it again!" cried Ilva, spring-
ing to her feet. She seized the back of a chair
which stood between them and held it tightly with
both hands. "If I am rude," she said, looking
steadily at her friend, "it is you who make me
so."

"Oh, it is not of the slightest consequence," said
Signorina Zanova, who was now scarlet as the bows
on her sunshade, with unmitigated rage. "If I had
known you were already enamoured of the man, I
would have said nothing to you. *Addio, cara mia;*

a better temper to you soon, and a sunny wedding-day."

She flourished her parasol with the air of one who offers the last insult to an already infuriated foe, and left the room.

As a matter of fact, Nadrovine was not in the least a Don Juan. It was no especial question of morality with him, however. He was a rather cold, excessively refined man, who found no amusement in *liaisons* of any kind. He would have been equally amused and touched by Ilva's warm defence of him. Of this young girl he was especially fond. Such natures are more capable of comprehending and returning the affection of children than those which are more sensual; and Ilva was in truth a child as yet. She sat down, after Signorina Zanova had departed, at the window which she had opened, and began to go over the years since the day upon which she had first met Nadrovine. She had not realized until a few moments ago how much he had again become to her, in spite of their uncongenial conversation.

She thrust back angrily the idea which Nathali had forced upon her. It gave her the same feeling that possessed her when she found that her maid had tossed a nosegay into the slop-bowl. It was a very blossom-like sentiment which she had always cherished for Nadrovine, and she felt as though her friend had dropped it into a figurative slop-bowl.

IV.

It was only three days afterwards that Ilva saw
Nadrovine again. The countess had driven into the
village early in the afternoon to do some shopping,
and the good Herbert was indulging in her usual
four-o'clock siesta, shut into her own room.   The
house was very dark and cool and empty, and the
day outside very vivid and hot and crowded with
sweet sights and noises and perfumes,—the sounds of
birds and of the sea, the voices of children wrangling
good-humoredly, the fragrance of sunburnt fruit.   On
the eastern terrace the grass was blue with fallen figs,
and the orioles made golden flashes among the
pomegranates in the tree just outside the girl's window. She could see the clustering blossoms among
the roots of the orange-trees, and the twinkle of the
sunlight on the wings of the bees humming over
them.   All about and above and beneath her were
brilliant winged things, that dipped and glanced and
alighted and took flight again, and there were some
variegated butterflies that looked like living jewels.
The day seemed holding out its arms to her. She
took a big white sunshade whose rose-colored lining
appeared to blush for its unfashionable proportions,
and, lifting a book at random, went out into the
fragrant, vibrating glare, under the pomegranate-
tree, over the fig-strewn grass, up the rough stone
steps that led to the ruined temple on the olive-

crowned hill-top, and so into the temple itself. She
threw herself on the sun-bleached grass and lay down
upon it, leaning her head, with its cushion of burnished hair, against the old marble seat.

Everything gleamed tremulously through the
rising heat. The tall wild flowers and weeds
seemed shuddering against the violent blue of the
sky beyond. One of the slender Corinthian columns
which had remained standing, had wavy outlines, as
of a white, ever-ascending flame. The vast grass-
fields below rippled like another sea. So intensely
still was it, save for the sounds of leaf and bird and
waves, that she could hear distinctly the soft dropping of the ripe figs upon the thick turf and a bird
whetting its beak on a fallen marble capital near by.
She was very warm, and yet a purring wind crept
over her every now and then and kept the heat from
growing oppressive. She had a great flare of fire-
colored azaleas at her belt, and an intoxicated sleepy
bee had fallen into one of the gorgeous chalices and
droned and struggled intermittently with a palpable
affectation of energy. One of the orioles, which
were yet very tame, poised on delicate, whirring
wings and tore at the red petals mischievously.

She did not even open the book that she had
brought with her, and she had been thinking of Nadrovine for some moments, when he spoke to her.
He had been watching her just as he had done
seven years ago, and, as he had also done on that

4

occasion, had mistaken her shut-eyed quiet for sleep. She rose to her feet with a supple, unhurried grace which did not escape him, and put up her hand to her hair,—the instinctive gesture of a woman whose hair-pins are forsaking her.

"I wish you had been soliloquizing this time also," he said, with a smile, as he stooped to lift her shawl and book from the grass; and then Ilva was very glad that her umbrella was lined with pink, for she felt herself redden a little.

"And I am thankful that I was not," she answered, candidly. "I am not much wiser than I was seven years ago, and I might have uttered just some such nonsense."

"I assured you then that I did not think it nonsense," said Nadrovine, gravely. "I do not think so now; and I remember it perfectly, word for word. You were wondering how it would feel if one were a giantess and had a giant lover to whom one could say——"

"Pray don't repeat it," exclaimed Ilva, with an imperious gesture.

"But if I think it charming?" said Nadrovine.

"That is impossible," she said, smiling all at once. She had one of those full, lissome mouths which adapt themselves exquisitely to a smile. Her whole face changed with it as water under a float of sunlight. The contour became more childish, and yet somehow her expression was more that of a woman.

She sat down suddenly on the marble seat and drew aside her white skirt to make room for him.

"Let us talk," she said, impulsively. "I have some things to say to you."

"It would take many hours to say all that I wish to say to you," replied Nadrovine, seriously. "In the first place, do you still write?"

He had taken his place by her, sitting sidewise, with one elbow resting on the back of the bench and his hand supporting his uncovered head. With the other hand he clinked some pebbles together, as she remembered him to have done during that memorable interview. He had thrown his hat on the ground, but it had left a red mark across his forehead. His hair clung damply to his temples. Signorina Zanova's remark about the Greek god came back to her. It was the face of a Greek, certainly. Ilva had a cynical disbelief in deities. She liked to look at him, but, being afraid of seeming to stare, turned her eyes presently to the azaleas in her belt.

"Oh, yes, I write, sometimes," she said, rather vaguely.

"Only sometimes?" asked Nadrovine. "Sometimes is the arch-enemy of success; and I remember you very ambitious."

She lifted her eyes again to his face, and his met them.

"Perhaps I am ambitious now," she said, with a half smile.

"I am rather inclined to think it is not 'perhaps,'" replied Nadrovine. He was reflecting upon the loveliness of that direct, gentle gaze. Most of the young girls of his acquaintance dropped their eyes with a puppet-like certainty under an at all prolonged look, while others returned such glances too boldly.

She charmed him very much. He was almost afraid to allow the conversation to take a serious tone, for fear she would disappoint him. She was looking away again now. A little white butterfly had alighted on the laces above her breast, and rose and fell with her soft breathing, as daintily as a bird upon a wave.

"If you have a sweetheart, signorina, be sure that he is thinking of you," said Nadrovine, suddenly.

She turned her eyes from the sea to him with a rather startled look.

"Why do you say that?". she asked.

"Because a white butterfly has alighted upon your dress. It is a sure sign."

She glanced down, and saw the pretty thing opening and shutting its silvery wings with all the coquetry of a conscious beauty manipulating her fan. She breathed more gently than ever, in order not to disturb it.

"Is that a Russian superstition?" she said, after a moment.

"I really do not know," Nadrovine replied. "But

I seem to have heard it all my life,—and the one
about a bird flying into a room."

"What is that?" said Ilva.

"They say that it is a forewarning of death or of
a great sorrow.   Myself, I am not superstitious.
One night in Russia I heard a tapping at my window,
and, like the melancholy young man in Poe's romance,
opened it.   There was nothing so startling as a raven
outside, however,—only a little brown bird who had·
been attracted by the light.   I let him in, and, after
flying distractedly about, he made himself quite com-
fortable on the back of a tall chair.   Then three
more rapped and gained admittance, and all four
spent the night with me.   In the morning I fed them
and set them free.   But they seemed only to bring
me good luck.   I got many things that I wanted
soon afterwards."

"A nightingale flew into my room once," said
Ilva.   "He was so frightened, though, poor little
soul, that he killed himself by beating his head
against the wall.   It made me very sad at first;
but I reflected that he might have been put into
pasta by some peasant, and so was somewhat com-
forted."

"You call him poor little soul," Nadrovine observed, smiling.   "I see that we share a belief."

"Oh, there must be birds in heaven!" the girl exclaimed, quickly.

"And why not?" said Nadrovine.   "One knows

there are horses,—made of fire, but still horses. It seems to me that birds have quite as much right to be there."

"Oh, much more," said Ilva, gravely. "I am sure that there must be many of them."

"One might say that the angels were a species of fowl," continued Nadrovine, gravely. "In all the pictures they have great wings covered with feathers."

Ilva looked at him, still seriously, but her eyes laughed under their broad lids.

"I have always thought they must be so uncomfortable," she said. "One would have always to be considering them, like a court-train or a travelling-case."

"What a prosaic simile!" cried Nadrovine, and then they both laughed. It is as impossible for two people who have laughed together to remain ceremonious in manner, as for a person to maintain strict dignity during a first lesson on the violin.

The butterfly was alarmed into flight by the gay sound, but they moved nearer each other.

"I begin to recognize the little girl I used to know," said Nadrovine. "When I first saw you the other night I thought you had become very stiff and conventional and difficult. You were rather severe with me also."

"Was I?" said Ilva. "Well——" She paused, and looked at him, laughing somewhat. "I, too, thought you very disagreeable," she said.

"And I tried to be so charming."

"That was the reason, doubtless. If one wishes to be odious, one has only to try to be charming."

"And does your rule work both ways, signorina? If so, I shall begin to behave accordingly."

She looked at him again, and again laughed.

"I like you very well as you are," she told him.

"But you do not know me as I am," persisted Nadrovine: "you only know me as I seem. If you are as cynical as you used to be, I shall feel a dread of your knowing me better."

"As I used to be?"

"Yes, when you wrote that terrible sentence, 'Married love is like champagne with'——"

"Do not!" cried Ilva. "It is as bad to quote one's sayings to one, as to tell one that you once heard Patti or Scalchi sing the song that one has just sung."

"But tell me, then, signorina, do you still believe that?"

"I have no experience," said the girl, demurely. "Some day when I am famous——"

"Ah, then you do intend to be famous?"

"If I can. Now, there you have experience. Tell me, is it pleasant to be famous?"

Nadrovine changed his position before replying. He leaned forward, and, resting his elbows on his knees, fitted a blade of grass between his joined thumbs.

"I will tell you what fame reminds me of, doushka," he said, a little absently. "There is a picture by Van Dyck of Charles V. in the Uffizi in your Florence, that is my idea of fame. The king is in full armor, on horseback, and an eagle holds a wreath of laurel over his head. The eagle seems to me to be an admirable type of fame. When he finally consents to crown one with the laurel, he at the same time gives one a sharp dig with his mighty beak."

"I thought you had everything in the world," said the girl, impulsively. Nadrovine lifted his thumbs, with the carefully-arranged blade of grass, to his lips, and blew a shrill little blast.

"That reminds me so of my boyhood," he said, before directly replying to her. "I had an old nurse who used to make me those whistles by the hour. She predicted, by the way, that I should have nothing in the world that I wanted."

"But you have fame, success, renown?" said Ilva.

"Only a little of each, doushka." He called her by the uncouth term of endearment absolutely without thinking. She seemed as much a child to him as she had done seven years ago in her brown holland frock and flowing mane. But she was not as much a child: she was like a rose-branch on which some flowers are in full bloom and others yet in the bud. It remained for him to discover this, however.

"Only a very little of each," he repeated.

" But," she said, with some impatience, " how can that be? You are known in many countries? Your books are translated into many tongues? You are honored and fêted wherever you choose to appear ?"

Nadrovine threw away the grass-blade and turned towards her, again running his hand deep into his curls and so leaning upon it.

" Does it not occur to you, signorina," he said, " that if my measure of success were quite full, its contents would not rattle so noisily ?"

" Bah !" said Ilva, with energetic rudeness, " that is unworthy of you ! That is fallacy. Why not be honest and acknowledge that you are famous and successful ? I should like you so much better."

" Would you ?" he said, a little curiously.

She had furled her big white parasol, and the brilliant sunset light was full upon her. Her spirited head was tilted rather imperiously backward. One could see the pulses of her throat stirring the lace of her white gown. Her hair and eyes seemed to concentrate the surrounding brilliancy.

" I should, I should," she assured him, vehemently. "·It is as false as though I were to look in my mirror and turn simpering away to murmur, ' How ugly I am !' "

Nadrovine looked at her, amused, but roused.

" So you do not make a secret of what your mirror tells you ?" said he.

"*Dio!* no! Why should I? I have eyes, and I have an excellent appreciation. It is absurd to imagine that I do not know I am handsome. There is this about it only. I do not admire myself. I am too slight, too pale. I like magnificent women, with brilliant coloring like an oil-painting. I am like a pastel. But because I and some others do not admire myself, is no reason why I should deny that I am handsome."

She paused, still looking at him, with her straight, dark brows drawn into a slight frown.

Nadrovine forgot for a moment that she was only a little girl of seventeen, she looked so thoroughly the woman, with her superb pose and air of displeased royalty.

"You have expressed it for me admirably, signorina," he said, at last. "I do not admire myself."

"Be honest, then, and confess that others admire you."

"Do you?" he said, smiling, but with quickness.

"Is not 'that a little impertinent?" she replied, but also smiling.

"Perhaps. But I was going to say that if you admire me I will confess myself a success."

"That is even more unworthy of you than several other remarks you have made this afternoon. I did not think that you would attempt flattery." She turned her head away, and he thought that she was angry.

"I am sorry if you think I meant to flatter you," he said, after a slight pause. "Are you very much vexed with me?"

"No, not vexed," she said, in a low voice.

"What then? Disgusted?"

"No, no," she said, hastily. Then, with a little movement towards her sunshade, which lay on the seat beside her, "Is it not getting rather late? Had we not better go in?"

A sudden thought struck Nadrovine.

"Doushka," he said, gently, "will you look at me?"

"I would rather, that is, of course," she replied, turning hurriedly. It was as he had thought. Great tears stood in her eyes. Nadrovine felt a strange stirring in his breast. He let slip all his chill delicacy of manner, while the blood sprang into his face.

"I beg you to forgive me. I beg you to forgive me," he said, unsteadily. "I forgot for a moment that I was not talking to a woman of the world, who would know how to accept such an absurd speech for its worth."

Had he wished this time to utter the most insidious piece of flattery in his power, he could not have reached the desired result more completely. To be mistaken for a woman of the world is as delightful to a young girl as for an older woman to be likened to a child. Her beautiful, luminous eyes did not fall from his.

"One hates to be flattered by those whom one es-
teems, as much as one likes to be flattered by those for
whom one doesn't care," she said. "When one doesn't
care, one laughs for thinking how silly people can be, to
fancy one is going to believe such words, and so amuses
one's self. But when one does care, it is different."

Nadrovine got to his feet and walked to the edge
of the little bluff. He stood there a few moments,
and then came back to her.

"I will not say all to you that I feel," he said,
looking down at her, "lest you think me crazy. But
will you tell me that you have forgiven me?"

"Indeed, indeed I will," she said, happily. "I
do not think you will ever speak so to me again."

"No, I do not think it likely," replied Nadrovine.

Ilva was very light-hearted the rest of that evening and all the next day. She felt that Nadrovine
comprehended her better than at first and would not
hereafter treat her so entirely as a child. She got
out the different notices of him and read them over.
What a brilliant man he was, after all, and what
exquisite romances he wrote! She buried herself in
a hammock and read one all day. It was as though
he were speaking to her. She recognized one or two
things that she had already heard him say.

V.

Nadrovine tried to analyze the feelings which had
possessed him when he saw the tears in the girl's eyes.

It escaped him, however, as a float of light escapes a child's grasp, falling each time outside of the fingers that would seize it. He was entirely conscious of the light, but it danced elusively and would not remain still to be analyzed. He realized only one decided emotion, the wish to see the eyes again, and—alas for the humanity which in his romances he so lauded !—to again behold them full of tears.

Had she been the ordinary type of a pretty, unsophisticated young girl, the tears would have signified to him mere moisture. But she was so extremely removed from anything ordinary that they occupied in his mind a place as unique as the drops which the fairy hung in every cowslip's ear. How vigorous and spirited she had looked while pouring forth all that tirade against him ! She reminded him of a young Caryatid who was fully capable of supporting the temple of her convictions. He was not, as a rule, fanciful, but he fell to wondering how her lovely curves would express themselves beneath the folds of a Greek peplos. There should be a crown of red roses on her hair, some of their shaken leaves upon her breast, one of her long white arms sunk deep into thick grass. Some one said of Vernet smoking, " Pif! paf! pouf! and he makes a man." " Pif! paf! pouf!" and Nadrovine made a goddess.

Not content with that, he fashioned a sultana, whose great, violet-gray eyes were like rain-washed amethysts. He surrounded her with Circassian girls,

c   d   5

who fanned her with wonderful plumes that leaped like flames from long wands of ivory. He went further, and created a little Russian, whose heavy hair drifting over her dress of palest blue and pink was as sunlight athwart the late sky outside.

Nadrovine was as fond of dreaming with his eyes open as are all who will acknowledge it. There was not a pretty woman of his acquaintance whom he had not espoused in imagination, and from whom he had not divorced himself the following day, or week, or month, as the case had been. One would have annoyed him in his writing-hours, one would have expected too much, one had coarse elbows when she took off her long gloves at a dinner. All made him smile. Ilva, on the contrary, made him frown,—a perplexed frown. She would probably never annoy him in his writing-hours, as she wrote herself. Her elbows were as complete as flowers. Then he had always remembered her with a tenderness which now made itself remembered in turn.

He leaped to his feet all at once and became very serious. He would not allow himself to think of her in a light way, no matter how pure. He had respected her as a child; how much more should he respect her as a woman! For she was a woman, he told himself, although the ghost of her child-self haunted her voice and speech and gestures, even at times the expression of her face.

She had occupied always a high place in his

thoughts. She should occupy one higher still, and in mounting to her new position she should close the door of her past dwelling behind her, as the chambered nautilus closes the door of its old habitation. She should become to him the type of noble womanhood, his Madonna Mia, whom he would help along the gracious ways wherein her feet were set. He was not thinking of love, the love that leads to marriage. Custom and a corrupt society had given him rather a gross idea of such love. He would never attempt to catch this Psyche by her wings, but would make so alluring the gardens in which he walked that she would alight among his flowers of her own free will. Theirs would be an ideal love, the winging of two souls to one object. He had entirely forgotten for the moment that Etiquette rules in Demeter's place, and that even souls are not undiscussed of domestics.

Nadrovine was not rich. He was, in fact, rather poor, although he would inherit great wealth on his mother's death. His poverty, however, was in a great degree the result of carelessness. He made and spent money with equal ease. He decided now that he was thoroughly capable of supporting a wife, should he ever look upon such a possibility as serious. The girl passed and repassed before him. Again and again he saw her tear-filled eyes. The faint perfume of the azaleas at her belt disturbed him. He seemed again to hold her hand,—the pliable, lovely hand, that had been so quiet, and yet so strong, within his. It was her latent strength, as much as her beauty, that he found enchanting.

At this point in his meditations he went and leaned over the terrace of the villa at which he was stopping, and looked down into the sea. The night was very sultry, and the whisper of the water sounded like an invitation. Nadrovine was much given to nocturnal swimming. It was long past midnight, and no one besides himself was awake in the house. He went down the sea-steps, after fetching his bath-sheet, and plunged into the tremulous net-work of moonlit ripples. Even this did not change the tenor of his thoughts. As the cool waves caressed and clasped him, he found himself wondering if Ilva Demarini were a good swimmer, and, if such were the case, how delightful it would be to cleave that gleaming highway which led even to the portal of the rising moon, with her beside him. He could fancy her flower-like limbs in their drenched white garments, and the flow of her radiant hair into the flow of the sheeny water. She would turn her noble head every now and then and smile and speak to him. If she grew tired, she should give herself into his arm, and he would swim with the other and so sustain her.

"I am thinking a great deal about that young girl," he said to himself, with some wonder, as he resumed his clothes and returned to his room. He went and lifted her silver book from a carefully-locked case which stood on his writing-table, and, seating himself, began to mark such passages as he considered appropriate for her to read. He was familiar with Ariosto, but re-read many stanzas, with that added interest which we always take in the pre-imagined appreciation of another.

When he next called at the Villa Demarini, not only was he told that the countess was out, but that the signorina had gone for a walk. As he passed along the terrace on his way back, it suddenly occurred to him that he would rest for a few moments among the ruins of the little temple on the hill-top. He found there a palm-leaf fan, a scarf of some gauzy, smoke-colored material, and the second volume of Taine's "English Literature." He lifted his brows a little as he took the book into his hand and began turning the leaves. As he glanced over the pages, some words scribbled in pencil caught his eye. He paused and read them. They were written at the end of the chapter on Ben Jonson, and were referred by an asterisk to the sentences regarding the complete idea which "conceives of the entire animal, its color, the play of the light upon its skin, its form, the quivering of its outstretched limbs, the flash of its eyes, and at the same time its passion of the moment, its excitement, its dash."

"This is surely very strange!" Ilva had written. "When on the other page Taine spoke of the ordi-

nary mind trying to imagine an animal unseen of
actual eyes, I closed mine, and, for example, imagined
a tiger (a beast which I have never seen). I saw
—nay, I heard the crisp crackling of the jungle reeds
and grass, with their russet-verdant lights filtering
through, the water curling among the thick blades
and stems, the flash of ragged and tawny reflection
as the great beast came padding through, the serrated
edges of the stiff blades dragging along his sleek
sides, the play of light among the supple wrinkles of
his hide, the darkening and yellowing of the great
eyes as his pupils contracted and dilated at the sight
of a drinking form. More than this, I felt with
him, marked the angry jerking of his tail's tip, and
the sheathing and unsheathing of his bluish-brown
claws in the oozy soil."

These hastily-scrawled sentences had a subtle
charm for Nadrovine, they were so entirely different from the sentiments which most young ladies
scribbled on the margins of their favorite volumes.
Had Ilva ornamented the margin of the pages with
many a "Bella! Superba! Bellissima!" it would
have seemed to him only the natural result of a
young girl's perusing so vivid a book. This account
of a mind-seen tiger aroused his surprise and a decided degree of admiration. He felt that his interest
in her was a crescendo, where in all other cases it
had been decidedly a diminuendo. "Without doubt
this little girl has a singular fascination for me," he

said to himself, impatiently. "I come to call. She is out. I am conscious of actual disappointment. I take up a book she has been reading, see some words that she has written on the margin, and thrill like any school-boy over the autograph of his first flame. I wonder if it can be possible that I——Ouph! I am idiotic! I shall go and begin work on that twenty-third chapter." As he was setting forth with this laudable determination, however, there came to him a sound of voices laughing, voices that approached nearer each moment, and as he stood at the top of the stone stair-way, Ilva appeared at the foot with a pretty child astride of her shoulders. Its small hands were clutched in her riotous hair, and her white woollen gown, full of wild flowers, was pinned up about her waist. She held the child's dainty ankles in one shapely hand, and the other grasped several dolls and a straw hat with a gold-colored lining. As she bent her head in the effort of climbing the rather difficult steps, she did not catch sight of Nadrovine during her ascent, and the child was too delighted with her tawny-maned steed to take much notice of anything else. All the way up she chattered gayly:

"And you will tell me a story? and then we will have chocolate? and a ball? You will invite the orioles, won't you, darling cousine? and the lizards? Do you know their tails break off—snap!—if one tries to catch them that way? The olives are so

black now; but we can pretend they are dates.
Have you grapes, cousine? And the apricot I
gave you? Oh! and the little knives and forks?"

"Yes, yes, yes, to everything," replied the girl,
merrily. "But, darling, if you pull out all my hair,
there will be no golden wire to strangle the naughty
prince with."

"Oh! do I pull you, my very dearest?" said the
little rider, distressed; then, all at once breaking off,
"Look! is that the prince?"

"Who? where?" said Ilva, staring. Then she
too stopped. "Is it you?" she asked, and to her
dismay felt the warm color wrap all her face.

"Unless it is my doppelgänger," said Nadrovine,
gravely. "And so I am the prince who is to be
strangled with a golden wire? What have I done so
wicked as all that?"

"You will have to ask Lotta," said Ilva. "I am
only chief executioner. I am not informed about the
offences."

The pretty elf on her neck swung round in order
to look earnestly into her eyes.

"Oh, cousine!" exclaimed she, "but you do know
about the prince! He stole Nicoletta's sash to draw
himself up to Viola's window."

"That was indeed a crime," said Nadrovine.
"But why do you particularly strangle him with a
golden wire?"

"Oh, because—because—because it suits his com-

plexion," ended the elf, nodding triumphantly at
him. She was as unlike Ilva as possible. Her
dark hair, falling in dense, web-like masses about
her small pale face, had absolutely no reflections.
Her eyes were a clear sea-gray, with soft shadows
above and beneath them. She was exquisitely
formed, slender and graceful as a dragon-fly. In
her little white pinafore were three more dolls.

"You must introduce me to these young ladies,"
he said, smiling, and holding out his hand. The
small Lotta placed one of hers sedately in the clearly-
marked palm.

"This is the bride," she said, indicating a damsel
in white satin with a very fluffy coiffure and gigantic
flesh-colored kid arms. "She is to marry the
prince."

"Oh! then she must be Viola," said Nadrovine.

"No, oh, no, indeed!" Lotta assured him. "It is
Viola whom he loves only; it is Nicoletta whom he
is to marry."

"Ah!" said Nadrovine, seriously. "Then he is
rich?"

"No, no!" replied Lotta, vehemently: "it is
Nicoletta who is rich. Don't you see? Else, of
course, he would marry Viola."

"Dearest little one," said Ilva, "who taught you
all this? It isn't fair for Nicoletta to have all the
money."

The child looked at her shrewdly.

"Mamma has all the money," she said. "Aunt Anita has not a——"

"The apricot! I have dropped it!" cried Ilva.

Then, as the child ran after it, she turned impetuously to Nadrovine.

"Do not think I have been teaching her such things," she said. "I keep her with me as much as I can, but, do what I may, she sees too much of the servants."

"I never think anything of you but what you would like to know," said Nadrovine. She turned away towards the child, and wiped the fallen apricot on a handful of grass.

"Now we will have the feast," she said. "Ask Signor Nadrovine to gather you some olives, if you wish them."

He went to the gnarled olive-tree and returned with a handful of the shrivelled fruit, and in the mean time Ilva had set out the mimic repast on the old marble seat, with her lace-edged pocket-handkerchief for a table-cloth. The little set of red-and-gilt china glittered brightly in the afternoon sun. There were several dishes composed of a grape each, and Nadrovine cut the apricot, as Lotta directed, into three pieces. There was a lump of sugar for each of the dolls, and Lotta bit a corner from hers with her sharp little teeth, to offer Nadrovine.

"Who is the charming young lady in blue?" he asked, as he crunched this original gift.

"Who? Francesca? She is the Signora Marilli. She hates her husband dreadfully, and is in love with the prince, and flirts disgustingly, and——"

"Don't you think it is time to strangle the prince?" asked Ilva, who was seated on the dry grass, braiding up the abundant brown locks of Nicoletta. Lotta agreed that she thought it was, and, having risen, shook out her pinafore and said that she would go to prepare the place of execution.

"Get a nice long one!" she called to Ilva over her shoulder.

"To what does that refer?" said Nadrovine. Ilva laughed,—a little confusedly, he thought.

"Why, it is dreadful nonsense, you know," she replied, "but she is such a dear child. She means a strand of my hair."

Nadrovine regarded her absently while she drew out the glittering almost invisible filament from her masses of burnished coils. "And round his heart one strangling golden hair," he said, half to himself.

"Ah! Rossetti," said Ilva, with one of her swift glances. "I do not always understand Rossetti; but that is beautiful."

"It is profoundly true," said Nadrovine.

"What! you believe in the men who have died for love?" said the girl, smiling.

"Do not you believe it?"

"For love of themselves and of their own way, yes," she said, mischievously. "I don't believe in strangling golden hairs, though. But then one can't blame Rossetti for writing rather bitterly of golden hair."

"Why?" said Nadrovine, who had long passed the stage when he feared that her conversation would disappoint him.

"Why? That is evident, I think. Did he not lament his wife to such an extent that he buried all his manuscripts with her, and did he not afterwards have the poor woman disturbed in her grave that he might recover them, and found that her beautiful golden hair had grown all about them? Perhaps it is not true; but I have heard it many times."

"Then the strangling golden hair must have been true in his case. He died rather young, you know."

"Yes, but he died of insomnia."

"And don't you think a strangling golden hair would be very likely to cause insomnia?"

"I know that you are joking," said Ilva, lightly. "And it is useless to try to prove to me that men are faithful to their dead. They wear loyalty so many months, as women wear crape, and then take another bride, as a woman puts on colors."

"And you think all women faithful?"

"Not all, of course, but nearly all. Why, surely you will acknowledge that?"

Nadrovine looked down a moment into his hat, which he held between his knees.

"I will tell you what I think, signorina," he said.

"The most faithful thing, after a dog, is the woman whom one has ceased to love."

He liked to bring the blood-stain to her clear brow.

"One never ceases to love," she said, haughtily. "If one ceases, as you call it, one has never loved. One may have a passion, of course, and that may cease: I do not suppose you think of such cases?"

"Do you mean to say that if you loved once it would be forever?" said Nadrovine.

She remained quite still for a moment, leaning on her hand, with her long fingers sunk deep into her hair and her eyes on the sea. Presently she looked at him steadily.

"Yes," she replied.

Then said Nadrovine, in a voice not familiar to himself, "I believe that you would."

The old proverb about the devil may be applied to Love: speak of him, and he is sure to appear. He is a confirmed eavesdropper, and never hears his name mentioned that he does not hasten to the spot. The things that he overhears are generally so pleasant that he has never been broken of this reprehensible habit.

"I believe that you would," Nadrovine repeated.

"Of course; yes. Why not?" said Ilva, hurriedly, disturbed by the new note in his voice. "How long Lotta takes! Lotta!"

Nadrovine smiled, leaning his head back against

6

the marble seat. The leaf-shadows trembled across his throat, and it looked so sensitive in its brown clearness that the girl wondered the dancing flecks did not tickle him.

"Lotta! Lotta!" she called again.

"Now, if these were the days of Pan," said Nadrovine, looking down upon her, his smile gone, "do you know what would happen?"

"No," she replied, returning his gaze as if compelled, but with an unmoved serenity.

"Why, there would come a little faun, a charming little kid faun, out of the ilexes there, and he would flute away on his reeds until the dainty Lotta danced away on his arm, out of sight, out of hearing."

He paused, as if expecting her to say something.

"And then?" she asked, mechanically.

"And then," said Nadrovine, gravely, "then we could continue our talk together."

A gleam went over her face, like the reflection of a white bird's wing in shadowed water. She felt a rebellion against his words, and yet she wished that she had allowed Lotta to go with her nurse that afternoon. She answered, however, with perfect simplicity,—

"You do not like children?"

"On the contrary. But there are some things that I like better."

"Ah? It is that?"

"It is that, signorina."

She turned to him suddenly with all the frankness of a flower that wears the sky's livery and sees no presumption in the act.

"Dear Signor Nadrovine," she smiled,—he saw the light strike clearly through the opal brightness of her little teeth,—"can you mean seriously that it gives you pleasure to talk to me?"

Nadrovine did not smile in reply. He was very grave, and his eyes met hers in a level look.

"It gives me the greatest pleasure that I know," he answered, and their eyes held each other.

"You are very good," said Ilva, presently, in a low voice, possessing her eyes again. She held out both hands to Lotta, who had returned after arranging elaborately the place of execution, and pretended to let the child pull her to her feet.

"Why, you are quite a little Amazon!" said Nadrovine.

"Pouf! that is nothing," replied Mademoiselle. "I fence. I fence with Victor. I can do un, deux, un, deux, trois, doublez, dédoublez—*fendez-vous!* I fence better than many boys. They get so angry. They want to poke one. George—he is my other brother—said, 'Cré! cré!' to me one day when I disarmed him. He danced: he did, indeed. He looked very ugly. I said, 'I pity your wife, *mon cher,*' and was so calm that he would have liked to slap me. He would have slapped me if he had not known that Victor would tell and he would get slapped himself.

You see?" She bared one pale little wrist, with its purplish thread-like veins, and moved it from side to side, exposing the flexile muscles.

"It is like steel," she said.

Nadrovine examined it seriously.

"A kiss would make you a bracelet, mademoiselle," he remarked, finally. "And you fence with this elf's love-charm?"

She looked at him unabashed and unoffended.

"I fence well," she assured him.

"I do not doubt it."

"And I am learning Italian. Which do you like best, the way that Signorina Zanova says 'Cecilia,' or the way that Ilva says it?"

"How does—Ilva say it?"

"This way, as if it were sweet in her mouth,— 'Sheshilia.' I like that best. It sounds as though she kissed it before she let it get away."

"Yes, I like that best," said Nadrovine.

"Very well. And when I am grown I will fence with you."

"Ah, yes, but it must be with foils."

"Why?" asked the child, puzzled.

"Because, mademoiselle, to fence with a young demoiselle without foils is to commit a great indiscretion."

"Si?" said Lotta. She then carefully arranged Prince Zi-Zi's sash, and, being weary of the conversation, announced that it was time to strangle him.

"A strange game," observed Nadrovine, as he followed them to the place of execution.

"Yes, but not so strange as it seems until one knows," explained Ilva, somewhat hurriedly. "As soon as he is strangled he is supposed to come to life as a good prince, and to turn monk for stealing Viola's sash."

"It was Nicoletta's sash, was it not?"

"He becomes good,—a monk. We have a great rosary made of berries."

"A monk!" said Nadrovine.

His tone arrested the girl. She paused in her task of tying a slipknot in the strand of hair, and looked up at him. His eyes dwelt on the far sea-blue. She felt suddenly apart from him, as though the sea had broken through the grass and flowers between them.

"I wished to be a monk once," he said, turning to her at last.

"And now?" she said, gently.

"And now? Not always. Sometimes. Not always. It must be a peaceful life."

"After one has lived," said the girl. She regarded him with a serene wisdom in her large eyes.

"You do not think, then, that I would make a good monk, signorina?"

"Perhaps, after you have lived," she repeated, smiling.

"Is not that something like saying that one would make a good ghost?"

" Perhaps."

" If I were a ghost," he said, suddenly, " I would haunt you. I would be in the wind outside your window, and you should feel me in the mists rolling in from the sea. If things were not as I wished them, I would disturb you sadly. I would blow in draughts upon such cavaliers as I did not approve. I would give them rheumatism, influenza,—everything unlovely."

" In that case you would make a better monk than ghost, signor." She did not look in the least conscious, and arranged the golden noose about Prince Zi-Zi's neck with calm fingers.

" Perhaps," he said, imitating her enigmatical tone of a moment before.

VI.

They executed the poor Zi-Zi, had another feast, in honor of his revival, and then prepared to descend to the villa.

" But my story!" said Lotta, hanging back. "You haven't told me a story, dearest Cousine Ilva, and I feel so unsettled when we cease our play without a story. The day doesn't end right. It is as if the sun went down, splash ! like a sponge into the sea, and put everything out. When you tell me a story, I come slowly, slowly to the idea of going to bed, and then I put myself to sleep thinking about it."

" Can you refuse that?" said Nadrovine; and

Ilva drew the child to her and fondled her delicate cheek.

"Signor Nadrovine is the one whom you should ask," she said. "He is far cleverer than I about telling stories. People make books out of his stories."

"Oh! books!" said Lotta. "I have many books. What I like is to feel that it is coming out of your lips, quite, quite new, and that you don't know any more than I do what the next thing will be."

"The prettiest story that I ever heard as a little girl was told to me by Signor Nadrovine," said Ilva.

Lotta regarded Nadrovine with palpably increasing respect.

"If you would but tell me one, signor!"

"There is a charming one that I think of," replied Nadrovine. "It is called 'The Princess of the Silver Book;' and I do not know how it ends, any more than you do."

"Why, how strange!" cried the child. "Cousine Ilva told me a story once, and it had a name almost exact——"

"Ah! the poor, poor Nicoletta!" said Ilva. "We are trampling upon her. Poverina! There! there! Hush! You see she will cry, my sweet. You will have to console her yourself. She is such a mother-baby. There!"

Lotta received her suffering daughter and tossed her back and forth with an air of dainty matronliness

which reminded one of a peach-bough swinging a
blossom.

"Poor thing! poor thing!" she crooned. "But it
is her own fault. Nini asked her yesterday how her
migraine was, and she said she had quite recovered,
—that she never felt better. She should have said,
you know, 'Thanks, I am well, but not so well as
yesterday.'"

"Ah, yes; you must teach her that our Italian
ideas are not to be laughed at. But she must have
a new sash in place of the one that Zi-Zi stole away.
Come to my room quite early to-morrow; I have
one that I will give her,—such a pretty, rosy thing,
like a little strip of that pink sky there."

Ilva was hurrying on, delighted at having turned
the child's attention.

"Oh, dearest Cousine Ilva, thank you! Nicoletta
wishes to give you her hand. She is nearly spring-
ing from my arms with delight. I can scarcely hold
her. Dearest Cousine Ilva, do give her a *bacigno*,—
a wee, wee one. It will so please her!" She looked
on with the bland smile of motherhood during this
performance, and then, as she received the cheered
Nicoletta into her arms and settled her gauze skirts,
she said over her shoulder to Nadrovine,—

"It was 'The Prince of the Silver Book.' I had
almost forgotten to tell you."

For the second time that afternoon, Ilva felt her
self blush from forehead to throat. In spite of her

wish to appear unmoved, she hastened her steps towards the house.

Nadrovine questioned the child in his grave way. "That is a coincidence, is it not?" he said. "Was it a fairy-story? and was the prince happy in the end?"

"He was great; that is much better than being happy. Cousine Ilva says that it is much better."

"Would you rather be great than happy?"

"I should have to think about that," replied Lotta. "I do not always wish to do what I ought. But then to be great!—to have one's way always!"

"To be great," said Nadrovine, "means never to have one's way."

Lotta tried to subdue the incredulity that swept over her small face at this announcement.

"I tell you what I should like to be," she said at last, waiving the subject. "I should like to have an invisible cap. When people displeased me, I would put on my cap and serve them as I wished. Oh, the fun that I would have! Oh, the droll things that I would do! Oh!" She drew a long breath, and tucked Nicoletta under her arm in order to clasp her hands ecstatically.

"What sort of things?" inquired Nadrovine.

"Why, for instance, when mamma took me to church and the curé preached too long a sermon, I would pop on my dear little cap, and steal on tiptoe behind him, and pinch his nose together so that he would sound as though he were wheezing through a toy trumpet. Oh, the poor man! how comical he would look! And then when they sought me, there I would be as still as a mouse, and the little cap in my pocket. Oh, I would rather have that than the big gold cross on the Madeleine, and a queen's crown, and diamond shoes, and live dolls! Cousine Ilva's prince wasn't at all like that, though. He was of a great dignity, and always spoke in a gentle voice, and called people—the princess, I mean— ' doushka.' That means ' little darling,' or ' dear little one.' He was the most charming creature. His eyes were of light, and his hair of sunbeams, and he always made people do good things without looking ridiculous. That is *so* difficult!" She sighed, and smoothed Nicoletta's hair.

"That must have been a beautiful story," said Nadrovine, feeling Ilva's embarrassment without looking at her, and hastening to change the subject. "I shall try and get your cousin to tell it to me some day."

"Oh, I am sure she will," Lotta assured him. "Won't you, cousine dearest? You would tell it now if we begged you, would you not?"

"It is too late. The story is too long. And there! there is Marie beckoning to you."

She kissed the child and gave her a gentle push forward towards her nurse, after waiting for her to make her stately adieux to Nadrovine.

Miss Herbert was sitting with her fancy-work on the terrace, and looked up as they approached.

"Has mamma returned?" asked Ilva, after greetings had been interchanged. "Is Aunt Cecilia in the drawing-room?"

No; Madame Boutry was still lying down, with a headache, and the countess had not returned.

"It is cooler out here," said Ilva, hesitating. She did not wish to seem to dismiss him, and yet she shrank from forcing herself upon him.

"Let us stay outside, by all means," replied Nadrovine. "The sunset will be superb, and I am sure poor Miss Herbert would dislike being dragged indoors."

"Shall we walk, or will you bring chairs?"

"Let us walk, if you are not tired."

"Oh, no! I am only tired of being still. I stooped too much over Lotta's dolls. It has made my head heavy. It will be delightful to walk."

"I brought your book with me. Shall I leave it with Miss Herbert? Or perhaps it is a copy that you do not wish to remain about the house. I had the indiscretion to read some of your marginal notes. You will forgive me? You know what an interest I take in your writing?"

She stood looking at him, stung by a rush of mingled sensations.

"How presumptuous, how silly, you must have thought me!" she exclaimed.

"Why, no.   It is a remarkable bit of writing, —terse, original.   If you are not displeased, I am delighted to have seen it.   You have great imagination."

"Do you think so?" said Ilva, in a low voice. Her heart seemed to shake her with its rapid beating, for his approval or disapproval meant much to her.

"Yes, great and original," replied Nadrovine. "You will let me see some of your manuscripts, will you not?"

"Some.   Perhaps.   They are very badly written. I have never shown them."

"I wish all the more to see them."

"Do you?" said the girl, for want of a better remark.   "It will be quite a task to read them.   They are written on both sides of the paper.   I believe that is a mistake."

Nadrovine was regarding her side-face as they walked up and down together.

"You are very serious in this," he said.   "It is a very serious thing to you, is it not?"

"Very.   I love nothing so much.   I cannot imagine life without it.   Do not encourage me to talk, signor, if you intend laughing at me.   I believe that you are in earnest, but I have no past experience by which to judge.   I have never spoken of this before to any one."

"I am sure you do not think that I would laugh

at you," said Nadrovine. His tone convinced her. She drew in a long breath of relief, and let it escape softly, that it might not sound like a sigh.

"It is very good of you to be interested," she said, in a restrained voice. "You must have so many people talk to you in this vein."

"On this subject; not in this vein."

"There are so many things that I should like to say to you, I do not know which to say first."

"I hope that you will take time to say them all, signorina. Believe me, nothing could delight me more."

"Oh, but there will not be time. I shall not see you often enough."

She paused, feeling that she had said something which had better have remained unspoken. She was too candid to try and escape by means of a subterfuge, and stood before him wordless, and too overwhelmed to do more than control her expression of dismay.

"I suspect you will see me oftener than you have any idea of," said Nadrovine, with ready tact. Her evident confusion was as delightful to him as the frankness of the silence which admitted it.

"You are very, very good," replied Ilva, and paused again.

She thought hopelessly of the conversations that would have to pass between them before she could speak to him without embarrassment, and tilted

her fine head with a certain air of restrained eagerness.

"I say nothing that I wish!" she exclaimed, impatiently. And then, before Nadrovine could correct
her, "I wish to tell you some simple thing, and I
deliberately say something else. But I will tell you
quickly, before my tongue runs away with the words,
how I thank you for your good words. They encourage me. They are much to me. I have read
all your books. Herbert has them. I have marked
some of them with my thumb-nail. Herbert will
not have pencil-marks in her books, but she does not
notice the nail-marks. Some of them made me
breathe as though I had been running. The one
where they take away poor Sovosky's dog at the
Siberian frontier, and one of the soldiers kicks it,
and it whines and tries to get to Sovosky, and
the soldier kicks it again and breaks its leg,—my
face stung when I read that. I hated that soldier. I could see the dog, and poor Sovosky with
the tears freezing on his face. Tell me," she
continued, eagerly, "did you ever see a scene like
that?"

Nadrovine paused a moment before answering
her, looking down at the grass between them, and
her high-curved foot sunk into its soft mat. Then
he lifted his eyes to hers.

"My father is in Siberia," he said.

Ilva pressed her hands together, feeling the same

hot smarting in her face that had stung her when reading of Sovosky and his dog.

"Siberia? Your father? He is in Siberia?"

They stood in silence, looking out over the sea, where in swirls of citron and vermilion a few sails were dissolving like feathers thrown against flame. Presently she said, in an undertone,—

"I do thank you for telling me that. I feel it. I feel it so much more than I can say. I cannot say how much."

"I can feel how much," replied Nadrovine.

A long, narrow veil of sea-blue gauze that she held over her arm blew out and clung to the cloth of his sleeve. It was like a visible sign of the airy thread of sympathy and confidence connecting them. He could have kissed it, so strongly had his feeling for the girl grown in this short, unlooked-for interview.

"You must not think that I told you this to harrow up your feelings and make you sorry for me, signorina. To be true, I love my mother best, although I always looked upon my father with an almost awed admiration. It will explain to you many things in my books which might otherwise seem unnecessarily bitter,—this fact of my father's exile, I mean. My mother has borne it more bravely than I have. She is very wonderful. You will like each other, I am sure. I am sure, at least, that she will like you; and she is very beautiful."

"If she will let me like her," said Ilva, hesitatingly. "The friends of friends are so apt to be enemies, and one's mother so rarely likes the people whom one is fondest of."

"My mother and I are the exceptions that prove your rule, signorina."

"You always agree?"

"We have never yet disagreed."

"And she is beautiful? Is she at all like you? I mean, is she dark or fair?"

"She has ink-black hair, and emerald eyes, and a skin like milk. She is nearly as tall as I am,—too tall, say the little men and women. She is five foot ten, supple and majestic, and with such a sweet voice."

"Oh, one does not care whether a woman is tall or short, if her voice is sweet," said Ilva. "Then you must be like your father? And was he tall also?"

"Two inches taller than I am. You will think us a race of giants."

"How lovely she must be, with her sweet voice!" sighed the girl. "I do not wonder that you worship her." The Countess Demarini was short and rather stout, and her voice, when she took the trouble to speak, had an asthmatic wheeze that gave way occasionally to a complaining whine.

"You have her picture?" continued Ilva, a little shyly.

"Yes,—two miniatures,—one in her Russian dress,

one in a black satin gown. If you would like to see
them——"

"Oh, yes," said Ilva, "please."

Nadrovine took out his watch, opened it, and held
it towards her. The face that she saw enthralled
her. It was of a long, oval contour, clearly pale,
save for the scarlet of the full, round lips, surmounted by night-colored hair, and made brilliant
with dark-green eyes slightly prominent under thick,
heavily-curved lids. The nose was short and well
cut, the ears symmetrically placed and clasping closely
the small, self-possessed head, the forehead high,
boldly modelled, shaded by a few short curls melting
into a violetish haze at the temples.

The pretty Russian head-dress set with pearls
and emeralds brought out vividly the tones of this
charming face.

"How very beautiful! How you must love
her!" cried Ilva. "And how young she looks!"

"Yes," replied Nadrovine, also gazing at the
miniature in the young girl's palm, "she has a remarkable appearance for her age. That miniature
was painted only two years ago; and she looks no
older now. I am glad that we agree in this instance
as well as in many others, signorina. I will tell my
mother of your approval. She is coming shortly to
Italy to spend the rest of this year with me."

Ilva turned on him her wide, clear gaze.

"Then I may see her; we may know each other.

7*

But I am afraid that young girls bore a woman like Madame Nadrovine."

"Perhaps," said Nadrovine.   "*You* would not bore her."

"Ah, but how can you tell?"

"We agree so perfectly."

Ilva looked once more at the miniature that she held, and then returned him his watch.   It was warm with her hand, and he kept it in his own for a minute or two.   The western light was in her eyes and on her hair, and a sweep of mystic rose-gray throbbed behind her.   She was still looking at him.

"I cannot tell you how kind I think you for the interest that you have shown in my work, in my wish to work," she said, rapidly.   "I know how very, very pale my hopes and ambitions must seem to you,—to you who have accomplished so much. I do not wish to say too much, to be what Herbert calls 'gushing,' but I do wish you to know that I appreciate all that you have said to me of kindness and encouragement."

"It is you who have been kind to me," replied Nadrovine.

"But the whole world is kind to you.   It is nothing for one unknown person to like what you write, and it is everything for me,—your approval, I mean.   I shall work so hard now.   I seem to feel a new zest: I am already longing to get my pen in my fingers. I may have something that I shall not feel ashamed to show you, after all."

"I shall wish to see whatever you have written. Believe me, I speak honestly."

"Ah, well, I cannot destroy your ideal of my power by doing anything so rash as that," said Ilva. She laughed a little, and drew the dim blue veil about her head and throat. He thought that her eyes must be like the eyes of Pandora before she had opened her box. "Perhaps she too picked the lock with a pen," he reflected.

"There is one thing that I must tell you before I go," he said, suddenly. "You will think me trite, and possibly morbid."

"What is it? Say it," returned the girl, with her eager imperiousness.

"It is this: that writing is a hard art. One has to suffer,—especially a woman,—especially a woman who has the courage of her opinions."

"That means that you think I have the courage of mine, does it not, signor?"

"I do think so, assuredly."

"But, then, if I am willing to suffer?"

"We are all willing to suffer as long as suffering means a vague pain which does not disturb our poise, or individuality, or surroundings. Ask yourself how you could bear to part with one of your hands."

She lifted one of her delicate hands, held it between herself and the fading sunset, and hesitated.

"The idea of being maimed is always so horrible."

"There are worse things than losing one's hand, doushka."

"What is worse?"

"To have the eye of the public always at one's key-hole. A man might go mad for that, thrust his pen through the opening and put it out, and so have no readers for his manuscripts. The sensation of being eternally pried upon,—there is nothing much worse than that; and that is the penalty."

They were silent for a few moments, and then Ilva said, with a gentle dignity,—

"I will remember. I thank you for telling me."

She turned, and Nadrovine followed her to the piazza, before which the Countess Demarini's carriage had just stopped.

VII.

Nadrovine was candid enough with himself to acknowledge, as he drove back to his lodgings, that he was interested in the girl to an absorbing degree. She had for him, in contrast to all other handsome women who had attracted him, that subtle charm which one only recognizes after one has yielded to its spell. She seemed to him as graciously and serenely pure as her own eyes, and as vivid in her unusual naturalness as their changing lights. It was perhaps —or rather probably—the fact of her mother's being an American that gave her the untrammelled grace of gesture and expression which so delighted him,

and she had evidently been without guidance save
that which the long-suffering Herbert had ventured
to exercise. He was also keenly conscious of the
subtle flattery contained in the disclosures of Mademoiselle Lotta. He had evidently been the hero of
all the young girl's day-dreams. She had thought
of him constantly, and he represented to her the
entire world of men. Nadrovine had always cherished an aversion to marriage. He felt this aversion
melting away as he fancied those quiet eyes transformed and wavering with the love-light that he
should have kindled, those lips so placid and undisturbed in their delicate curves trembling with words
of confession. He did not realize how intensely her
individuality had impressed him, until in his conjec-
tures he found himself wondering what type of man
would finally win and marry her. He shrunk from
it as sensitively-organized people will sometimes
shrink from throwing a flower into the fire. There
was no man of whom he could think as husband to
that slender, Psyche-faced child without a shudder of
revulsion and apprehension; for he was one of the few
men who recognize that a woman may be married
while her soul remains unwedded, and that the fate
of the victims of the Minotaur was preferable to this.
He realized that the only love to which such a woman
would yield would have to be as supreme in its reverence as in its fire, a white flame, still, pure, and ever-
ascending. Her dreams would be a man's only rival;

j

but then few have ever estimated the force in the
rivalry of an ideal.   The man who is measured by a
woman's imagined lover is far less fortunate than the
man who has to deal with an actual being.   Nadro- .
vine recognized all this; but underneath and ever
present was that consciousness of having dominated
those girlish dreams, of having figured as "The
Prince of the Silver Book."

He was often at the Villa Demarini during the
next fortnight.   Sometimes he would see Ilva, generally in the presence of her mother and Miss Herbert;
while once or twice he had the good fortune to find
her alone with Lotta among the ruins of the little
temple on the hill.   She finally consented to show
him one or two of her manuscripts, and he was singularly haunted by them,—vigorous original essays and
poems, decidedly ungirlish in their handling of sub-
jects which she could only have imagined.   He saw
that there was genius throbbing under the crude
richness of language and ideas, and told her so.
She did not say much, but the look in her eyes was
sufficient.   He was beginning to tire of seeing only
gratitude and appreciation in those clear eyes.   She
seemed made for love,—the love of a man who has
recognized-that God created him for one woman and
who has lived his life with a view to their ultimate
meeting.   Nadrovine had so lived his life, and the
girl was growing inexpressibly dear to him.

He had the good fortune to find himself beside

her on horseback late one afternoon in June. They were on their way with Miss Herbert, Lotta, and her two brothers to visit an old castle belonging to a cousin of Count Demarini, a haunted place which boasted murders and blood-stains, and, best of all in the eyes of the two boys, underground dungeons with great stone doors. They were wild to inspect these gloomy places, and chattered of them all the way over.

"What strange creatures boys are!" said Ilva to Nadrovine. "They seem to delight in all sorts of cruel, grewsome things!"

She was dressed in an English riding-habit, sitting square and straight on her neat hunting-saddle, and riding a handsome chestnut with one white hind stocking and a star between his eyes.

"I confess that I don't like boys," she added, pausing as though to wait for his expression of disapproval.

"Sometimes one finds a boy whom one loves," replied Nadrovine, "but it is very rare. The two little animals in front are very pretty, with their blue eyes and blond hair, but they are little animals for all that."

"So different from Lotta. She is like a sweet fairy," said Ilva. "And how deliciously she manages her pony! One wants to take her, pony and all, into one's arms."

"She adores you."

"Yes; she has a great ideal of me. I fear for her when it is dispelled. It takes a great deal of self-control to live up to a child's ideal of one."

"Or a woman's," said Nadrovine.

"Do you think that many women have ideals of men, nowadays, Signor Nadrovine? I know very few women, but those that I do know seem to me hardly to do men justice."

"That is perhaps the reason, signorina, why we do not live more nobly. We know that most women do not expect it of us."

She turned on him her frank smile and the glow of her believing look.

"Why do you say such things, except in your books? I know that you have lived nobly."

"I was only speaking of men as a class. I have had my mother's belief in me to live up to. I owe much—nearly everything—to my mother."

"She must deserve your worship, signor."

"You will think so indeed when you know her. I expect her next week. I am like a lover awaiting his lady,—as restless and nervous as a boy."

"It must be almost divine to a mother to have such a love," said the girl. "It is the most beautiful love of all. Do you not think so?"

"No, signorina."

"You do not?" She flushed a little, but asked her question bravely.

"No, doushka; there is one love which, when it is

as God meant it to be, is more godlike than any on earth. The love of Christ for the Church is not compared to the love of a father for his child."

"No?" said Ilva. She could control her voice, but not the violent leaping of her heart.

"Can't we ride faster?" here called Miss Herbert, who, unlike most Englishwomen, did not ride well, disliked a trot, and was only happy when cantering. "We can see nothing of the castle before sundown if we do not hurry."

"There will be a moon," said Nadrovine under his breath.

His heart was beating rapidly also, and he wished poor Herbert in many an unpleasant place.

"Yes, nearly a full moon," said Ilva. They set their horses in a gallop and soon overtook and repassed the others.

"How you would enjoy a ride over the steppe!" said Nadrovine, as they drew rein. "I can see you on a black Russian horse with your hair loose."

"Oh! oh!" said Ilva, relieved at finding an excuse to laugh. "One never rides with loosened hair except in Perrault's fairy-tales. Fancy how slovenly one would look in a top-hat with one's hair flying!"

"I was thinking of the contrast between the horse's mane and your hair. You have such wonderful hair. It is like a little child's, and it is so thick. It must weigh your arms down to comb it out."

"Ah! here we are at the gate," said Ilva. "What

hideous stone griffins! but the gate itself is beautiful."

"There are three more miles through the
grounds," called Miss Herbert. "We must hurry,
my dear!"

They galloped up to the door of the castle. It
was a great square pile, draped with vines, and surrounded by huge cedars and olive-trees. They were
shown over it by the cicerone, a withered creature
with dull eyes and an even duller mind. He had
not a word to say, but threw open doors on gloom
and beauty alike with the same unvarying stolidity
of countenance.

They were retiring rather disappointed with their
jaunt, when Victor and Georges precipitated themselves at the same time upon Miss Herbert, crying,
"The dungeons! the dungeons! We must see the
dungeons!"

"Well——" said Miss Herbert, weakly.

"Do you care about it?" Nadrovine asked Ilva.

"Now that we are here, we might as well see
them," she replied; "and the boys seem beside
themselves."

It was therefore decided that they should visit
the dungeons. Pietro, the cicerone, arranged a very
mediæval-looking torch in a species of iron cup, and
prepared to lead the way.

"Why don't you take a lantern?" asked Nadrovine.

"We have no lanterns, Excellency," replied the automaton.

"Then a candle or a lamp?"

"Candles and lamps blow out, Excellency."

"In that case, your idea of the torch is capital," said Nadrovine, dryly; and they all laughed,—all except Pietro, who descended the narrow stairways like a statue in motion, with no expression on his face whatever, either of amusement or distaste.

There were four of these underground cells, each damper and more slimy than the last. The mud seemed to be at least an inch thick on the soggy floors, and the slime clung in ropes to the trickling walls.

"Let us go in, just to say we have been in," urged the boys; and so all six went and stood in the hideous place, shrinking involuntarily from the coated roof and sides. The doors were of stone a foot thick.

No one spoke.

"Three men were starved to death in there, so it is said," droned the cicerone, giving voice to his first remark. He would not enter, but stood just without, thrusting his torch back and forth and waving it about to give them a full view of the horrors which surrounded them. They started. It seemed almost like the utterance of a ghost. The only unimpressed beings were the two boys, who flitted in and out like will-o'-the-wisps, their fair hair seeming to catch fire from the fitful torch-light.

VIII.

No one could quite tell how it happened. There seemed to be a sudden scuffle, a sharp cry from Pietro. The torch fell hissing in the mud just beyond the great door, and the door itself closed with a heavy jar. Everything at once became quiet. No sound reached them from the outside. In the ooze of the floor the great knot of resinous wood lay sputtering and sending up a heavy coil of smoke. The faces of the four who were shut in were seen wide-eyed and strained in the dull glow. Miss Herbert drew Lotta up into her arms and pressed the child's face down upon her shoulder.

"Victor! Georges!" cried Nadrovine, "open at once!"

He struck the stone with his hands. No grave was ever more silent than the place into which they had been shut. The fallen torch smoked on slowly to its final spark, and the cell was filled with the tarry smoke. Then a thick, soundless darkness closed about them. Lotta began to sob in a nervous ecstasy of fear.

Ilva felt Nadrovine close at her side, though he did not touch her.

"I am not afraid," she said, before he could speak. "Shall we have to wait long?"

"I cannot tell," he replied. "Those little——" he addressed some terms to the sportive young

Boutrys between his closed teeth. "They should be soundly flogged," he ended. "I fear you will take a horrible cold in this vile den. Wait a moment."

Ilva felt something soft thrust under her feet; she trod upon it with a smile which seemed strangely unnecessary in that thick blackness.

"Is it not drier? You do not feel the damp so much?" inquired Nadrovine, anxiously.

She said, "No. I thank you so very much."

Lotta went on sobbing, and the sound was almost a relief to them.

There passed what seemed to them a long time.

"I have some matches," said Nadrovine. He struck them one after another until they were all gone, and looked at his watch.

It had been only four minutes since they were locked into the cell.

"This is terrible!" cried Miss Herbert, shrilly. "What can have happened? I will see that those boys have a just punishment,—a severe caning."

"And I!" said Nadrovine, grimly. They felt that Miss Herbert nodded approval before again bestowing her attention on the frightened Lotta.

The minutes slowly passed. Ilva could hear the loud ticking of Nadrovine's watch in the dense silence, and it seemed strange that it should continue on its way so calmly,—as strange as that the rich Italian sky swept cloudless overhead, and that the fair afternoon moved on to night uninterrupted.

"I can't understand why they do not let us out at once," said Ilva, finally. "Do you suppose that the cicerone does not know how to open the door?"

"It may not have been shut for many years," replied Nadrovine. "He may not understand how to unclose it. Are you cold? I seem to feel that you are shivering."

"You felt that? How strange! I was shivering; but I am not cold. After all, it is a grewsome feeling, being shut into a place like this."

Involuntarily they spoke in whispers and drew nearer to each other. Nadrovine was standing between Ilva and Miss Herbert, and put his hand on Lotta's little head to reassure her while he spoke.

"It cannot last more than ten minutes longer, at the utmost," he said. "Evidently the cicerone has gone to get aid of some kind. You must have conquered both Victor and Georges at fencing this morning, mademoiselle, to cause such spite."

"I f-f-fenced with Georges," sobbed Lotta, "and b-b-broke his f-foil, and then I made V-Victor angry b-by saying he would be a s-s-sneak if he told—if he t-told M-m-aman when Georges pushed me. Oh, will it be long, m'sieu? Please hold my other hand. Please hold me very tight, Mees Herbert. I wish you would tell me a story about light places, and sunshine, and bright blue and pink flowers! It will help me to compose myself. You know truly I believe myself to be dreaming." She fell into nervous sobbing again, and buried her head in Miss Herbert's shoulder.

"If one had only brought one's goloshes!" murmured that patient creature. "But, then, how could one imagine such a contingency? Hush, hush, my dear child! I will tell you a story, if you will only listen." She went off into a long, rambling narrative in which she and her four brothers and sisters all played conspicuous parts.

"You are still shivering. I am sure that you must be cold," said Nadrovine. "You are too near that damp wall." He put out his hand to ascertain her position, and it came in contact with her soft hair.

"If you would lean on me!" he said, in a low voice.

He found the slight, ungloved hand and drew it through his arm. "How you tremble, my poor child!" he whispered. "This will have a terrible effect on you."

She did not answer at once, and then said finally, in a low voice, "I am glad that you are here. I feel safe."

"Doushka!" he whispered, in an indescribable tone.

Ilva felt that a tremor ran through him also. She strove to control herself.

"I—I think if only Miss Herbert and Lotta and

I had been shut into this dungeon, that I should have
suffered a great deal. I think of all sorts of horrors.
I seem to feel those starving wretches crawling and
cursing in the mud at my feet."

. She felt herself drawn closer to him, a perceptible,
imperious movement.

" You are not afraid with me ?"

" No."

" You trust me ?—you believe in me ?"

" Yes."

" You feel that I would stand between you and all
evil ?"

There was a pause, and then she said, clearly,—

" I feel that."

" Ilva !" said Nadrovine. She felt his arms close
around her. She did not repulse him. His lips
rested against her forehead, and all the darkness
seemed to press in golden throbbings against her
closed lids.

She stood locked in his arms, wordless, for a long
while. They could hear Miss Herbert droning out
her chronicles of Matilda and Alfred and John and
Charlotte and their troubles with their kitchen-gar-
dens, and how they were paid fourpence for every
turnip that they brought to perfection, and sixpence
for every carrot, and how they discovered a new
species of rose by mixing the seeds, and how they
made enough money by it to purchase a brass lectern
for a gift to their father on Michaelmas, etc., etc., etc.

Ilva felt sure that Lotta was right and that they were all dreaming. Those quivering lips on her forehead were the only real things in this chaos of unusualness and living gloom.

As for Nadrovine, the past seemed to have broken in a mighty wave on the shore of the present, and to have left him stranded there. All his ideas and theories of the last ten years were no more in this surge of emotion than shells and strips of sea-weed on the actual sea. He knew that to clasp in his arms this fragile piece of girlhood, feeling her content to be there, was sufficient, and that the hope of sealing, on some future day, her pure and sensitive lips with his, held for him more possibilities of joy than were contained in the cup of fame pressed down and running over. He loved her as women should pray Heaven to be loved,—with a keen recognition of all the traits that he did not himself possess, and a determination to consider them most when he understood them least,—with a reverence as intense as it was sincere for the child in her, which is part of every complete woman, old or young, an absolute belief in her delicacy of soul and body, an adoration of her very self and spirit, which constrained him rather to imagine the love as seen in her eyes than as felt on her lips, and an awe for her purity which made him think that, while as her lover he might dare to caress her mouth, as her husband he would only venture to kiss the utmost edge of her garments.

In a few moments more the door was opened for them.

It was as Nadrovine had thought: the cicerone had had to procure the aid of two other servants before he could move the heavy block of stone. Victor and Georges were scampering homeward, in dismay at what they had done.

Nadrovine and Ilva rode forth beneath a sky which seemed to float like a golden bubble above them,—a bubble blown upward from the great bowl of the earth which hollowed to the horizon. The pines seemed dripping with sherry.

"They are like green beards of Tritons drenched in wine," said Ilva, fancifully, as if speaking to herself.

Miss Herbert, urged by wrath, had for once conquered her fears, and had ridden ahead at a smart gallop to overtake and lecture the two culprits. Lotta at her heels on her Polo pony forced the pace, and they were both soon beyond sight and hearing.

Ilva, feeling Nadrovine's eyes upon her, moved uneasily in the saddle.

"Doushka, give me your hand," he said, at last.

She put it, palm up, in his.

"Do you give it to me really, my shy one? Is it mine to do with as I like?"

She could not trust herself to speak, but made a downward movement of assent with her chin.

"Then first," said Nadrovine, raising it to his lips, "this, and afterwards—this." He drew a ring from his own hand and pushed it firmly to the base of her slight finger, saying, in a low voice,—

"With this ring I seal thee to me. Thou art mine, my betrothed, my promised."

She trembled, and he released her hand.

"Will you see if you can read the motto cut in the stone, doushka?" he asked, after a long pause. "The light is fading, but the letters are very clearly cut. Try."

She held her hand towards the mellow tremble overhead, and read aloud, falteringly,—

"'Esto sol testis.' It is Latin, is it not? I do not understand Latin well. What is the meaning?"

"'Let the sun be a witness,'" replied Nadrovine. "Let a man strive to keep his life so clean and without reproach that the sun can search its every cranny without bringing unwholesome or ugly facts to light. It is not the family motto. It is the motto that I selected for myself and had cut in that sapphire when I was a boy of fourteen. I wish you to wear it now and share it with me."

He smiled, and, stooping, kissed the ring as it lay like a drop of blue sea-water upon her pale hand. "I wish the sun to be a witness to my love for you."

"Oh!" said the girl, dropping her reins and placing both hands against her throat.

The horses had stopped together on the crest of a little hill.

"What is it?" asked Nadrovine, quickly.

"Nothing. I love you so!" She leaned towards him, holding out her arms. Her eyes dwelt full and clear upon his. He bent to her, and she pressed his head against her for a moment, looking out over it into the red ball of the sinking sun that he had invoked to witness their betrothal. It seemed to her as though she were gazing through a flaming orifice straight to the core of heaven. Her heart was a prayer within her. It would have been almost a sacrilege to form words with her lips at that unspeakable moment.

They rode on in silence for a long while, until the last fires of the splendid, cloudless sunset were blotted out by the soft gloom of twilight gray as a moth's wing. The green lights of the first few stars shone down upon them through the rich haze, like glow-worms seen through a vast cobweb. Overhead was the sound of the wind in the pines and the call of the nightingales. The night opened about them like a great flower sleepy with perfume. They seemed folded in its warm petals,—a part of it,— as content as the small creatures that live in roses. He held her hand, and her life seemed flowing into his through that close clasp. He could not believe in a time when this proud sense of ownership, of duality, had not possessed him. The great, glorious, changing, growing night seemed without meaning save as a setting for that young creature at his side, with her hair which seemed woven of the spiritualized sunlight which one sees in dreams, and her eyes which seemed to hold all shadows and light, all love and pain, in their serene depths.

He felt that even pain with her would be outwardly a calm thing, a great stillness, as her love was now. But she spoke to him presently.

"I seem to have belonged to you always," she said, with her beautiful candor. "I seem only to have a right to myself through you. Your love makes me glad to be myself; because if I had been any one else, no matter how great or good, you would not have loved me, and your love is best. No, no: you must not speak; you must not contradict me. Just let me say what is in my heart. I feel that what is there must run into your heart like a stream into the great sea. It is wonderful to think that I have your love,—I out of the world! It is as though a great star were to concentrate its light all on some little flower, and say, 'I will shine only for this flower that I love.' It is as though some high one in heaven were to refuse to sing in the great choir, that his voice might be heard only in the dreams of some poor woman upon earth whom he loved and waited for. Ah, do not interrupt me! It is so big in my heart. It strains it. I have no one else to speak to,—indeed, no one that

I care to speak to. You are the only one,—the very
first,—the first since I was a little child and I gave
you my silver book. You helped to form my life.
You helped to make me into what you now love.
You were like a song through the silence of my life,
—like the song that Pippa sang so unconsciously,
always, always at the right moment. Always your
memory was with me at the right moment. I never
had a wrong thought, a wrong impulse, that your
face did not come to me as clear, as clear,—it was
as clear as that white magnolia flower there in the
moonlight. And your eyes would look so grieved.
I longed to ask your pardon, to have you take my
hand and say that you forgave me. I dreamed
about you sometimes when I was awake, sometimes
when I was asleep. When I used to fancy how it
would be if you were dead, it seemed to me that my
life would never stop going on, on, on, on. And
my heart seemed like a tiresome voice insisting that
I was alive. I would try not to listen to it.; but it
would seem to fill the room. And then I would lie
quite still and think, ' After all, it is you who love
him, my heart. Beat on, beat on! Oh, do not
stop! without you I could not give him my love.'

"And then I would imagine you married to some
one,—some one fair and tall, having great dark eyes,
and wonderful hair with deep shadows and lights,
like the lights on moving water,—some one whom
you loved. It was like a band squeezing my heart.

It was as though crabs had my throat and side in their nippers. I would get up and go to the window and fill my soul with the night. And then peace and rest and gentleness would seem to flow down to me through the stars, as though their rays were silver threads binding my soul to heaven. I would say, 'Perhaps it cools his eyes to take the stars deep, deep into them. Perhaps he kneels sometimes and looks up at them as I am looking now.' And then I would say, 'Give him peace too, dear stars. Give him rest, and a cool quietness, and thoughts of the shady places of heaven, as you have given me.' And then I would sleep. I was only a child; but I loved you. Oh, I loved you!—not so much as I do now, but much—much—— !"

She lifted his hand, and would have pressed her lips upon it, but he stopped her.

"Not that! not that!" He could not speak.

She waited for him, looking up at the gathering stars in mid-heaven. "My heaven-hearted one! my spirit-love!" he said, at last. "How am I to speak to you? How am I to put into my blunt man's words the story of my love for you? Let me prove it to you, beloved! Do not wait for me to speak. There is nothing that I can say after what you have told me. Even the passion of sunlight would seem too earthly after the starry sweetness of your words. You are all to me,—everything. You are sun and stars, the night and the day, the inland and the ocean, reality, dreams, ambition, fruition. You surpass my ideal, inasmuch as it is not in the power of a man, no matter how clean and high his life has been, to evolve out of sheer imagination a woman like yourself. Were a man, even faintly, to imagine such a woman, she would seem in his dreams unreal, evasive, cold. You are as real to me as music, as the May, as the light on summer hills, as warm as the heart of summer, sweeter, more full of possibilities. There is nothing chilling about you, and when I draw you to me, so, and feel your sweet life throbbing in my arms, I wish that day might never break again, but that we could live on in this trance of content, closed in by this vast night, watched over by the stars with their light in our hearts."

"My man of men," said the girl, "was I not right to love you?"

"You humble me! you humble me!" cried Nadrovine, passionately. "I had thought my life a clean one until your love shone on it. And now it seems full of dark places!"

"It is full of my love," she said, pressing her cheek to his, and touching his bended throat lightly with the ends of her long fingers.

"I cannot speak," he said. "Forgive me. I have no words. I have dreamed of such a love,—of such a love as I feel for you, I mean. There are no words. I will listen to you."

A lustrous quivering began to fill the air,—the

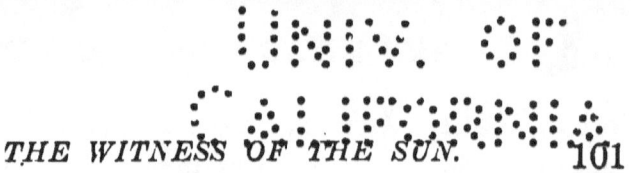
light from the rising moon. All things were radiant
with it. White flowers appeared here and there from
the shadows, as the stars had appeared at first in the
heavens. As the silver edge began to gleam behind
the almond-trees on a rise near by, she turned to
him with an exquisite shyness, lifting her face to his
in the tranquil light.

"Let the moon be a witness, also," she said, on a
catching breath; and, stooping, Nadrovine put his
mouth to the word-stirred lips. It was a kiss long
and gentle, but such a kiss as he would have given
a child. He could not have kissed her as a lover
then, even had she desired it. . But she smiled with
perfect joy, drooping her head a little, and grudging
even the night-wind its touch upon her lips.

They parted in utter silence, Nadrovine holding
her upon his breast a moment when he lifted her
from the saddle, and making silently the sign of the
cross upon her forehead.

IX.

Nadrovine was a man whose nature was too refined for his life to have been coarse. He was moral
rather from inclination than from principle; although
principle would have restrained him to a great degree even had his tastes been different from what
they were. Crime had no attraction for him, and
he would as soon have turned from galloping upon
elastic turf to plunge along through a muddy lane,

as to have turned aside from the pursuit of his art to accept caresses that bored him. There are such men. They are termed icicles by the ignoble and given small credit for their course of action. " We will give a tiger credit for not eating men," say the wise, " but a horse is graminivorous : why should we praise him because he does not feed upon flesh ?"

In truth, Nadrovine was not cold ; but the fires of his nature were as deeply buried as those of earth, and when they were quiescent ice and snow could form above them, and so the wise were deceived. The hearts of most men are like the grates in inns, where the wood is laid ready for kindling ; and the smile of any pretty woman is enough to set it in a blaze. Nadrovine's heart resembled a volcano, and it depended upon his own nature and the voice of one woman as to whether or not the hidden flame would be discernible.

To those who have an indomitable patience, love in its highest and most complete form invariably comes. Whether it be for pain or gladness, those who have dreamed loyally of Love, not condescending meanwhile to distract themselves with Philotes, will always feel, at last, his hands in theirs, and see the tears and laughter of his eyes. As Nadrovine rode slowly home beneath the tremulous splendor of the stars, yesterday seemed as far beyond him as though he had slept for a thousand years and been awakened by a kiss. He seemed always to have loved her,—always to have belonged to her, as she had said of herself in regard to him, with her pure frankness. In truth, it is never anything but what we have given up that comes to us. He had given up, long ago, all idea of bestowing or receiving love, and now his breast actually ached with a magnitude of devotion such as he had never ventured to describe, even in his most impassioned romances. Here was a love which seemed the beginning of everything instead of the end of a great many. Instead of resigning all other women in order to possess this one, he felt that in contrast with her all others ceased to exist. They became mere ciphers, which served to increase the value of his unit by passing behind her, and he wondered that he had not recognized in her as a child the spirit which as a woman would enthrall him.

He entered the cool hall of the pretty villa which he had taken in order that his mother might spend the rest of the summer with him. There was a heavy scent of roses on the air. An armful of the deep, orange-colored flowers lay on a low table under some wax-lights, and two or three had fallen on the red tiles of the floor. As he stood absently looking at them, the faint odor of a cigarette passed through a curtained door and floated towards him. At first he was scarcely conscious of it, then started, and, turning, entered between the curtains into the apartment beyond.

"Ah, at last!" was breathed rather than spoken.

His mother, leaning back among gold-colored cushions with a knot of the orange roses at her breast, reached up languidly with her beautiful, half-bare arms and drew his mouth down upon hers. The perfume of the cigarette-smoke upon her breath and in her hair irritated him, and the roses jarred upon him after the wonderful freshness of the night out-side,—being of the rare, hot-house species which one invariably associates with dinners and balls.

The slight shade of annoyance, however, only accentuated the radiant expression of welcome which had lighted his face when she first spoke.

"Have you waited long?" he said. "I did not expect you until to-morrow. Is your room in readiness? Have you as many apartments as you wish? Small one, how good it is to see you!"

She leaned over him as he knelt at her side, caressing his curls by nipping them with her lips which she drew in over her teeth, and pulling them so as to cause him a slight pain. His chin she had taken into one of her strong, flexile palms, so that he could not pull away, and her other hand was behind his throat.

"I have everything. I have you, my little dear one!" she replied. "It seems to me as though I can never forget that you were once my baby, and that you lay with your little face buried in my throat, and pinched me with your sharp little gums to show

when you were hungry. I feel you now,—no longer
than one of these roses, stem and all; and so soft!
You smelt always of ironed linen and dried violets.
I can sniff your little damp head on the flannel now.
And that is all gone forever! Vladimir, if you ever
marry I don't think I shall make a great noise. I
think I shall go very quietly to your bride's house
to take her a wedding-present; and when she is
asleep, with her white throat bent backward for
your dreamed-of kisses, I shall give it one snip, deep
to the left, with my little, crooked toilet-scissors, and
then strike her across the lips, very lightly, once with
my gloves. Come! How pale you are! How you
scowl, my great one! Come into your old small
one's arms and let her tell you that really your bride
shall be as her own child, and that she will kiss the
pretty throat and mouth many times for the kisses
that you will have left there. Ah!" she added,
pressing her lips again to his, " but it is absurdly
delicious to think that I am not called on to share
you yet,—that you are all mine,—all that you do not
put in those books of yours. But there is something different,—a look, a pose, a—I don't know
what. Is it a new book? Have you been writing
a love-scene?"

She drew back, pressing him from her with a hand
on either shoulder and regarding him steadily from
narrowed lids with her dark-green, jewel-like eyes.
" Ah, yes! you have been writing one of those de-

scriptions where one feels through the people one is writing of. You have trembled with your hero beneath the kiss of some beautiful woman. He has taken her in his arms, and your breast has throbbed. Go!—go and bring it and read it to me. I will not even smoke while I listen." She gave him a little push forward, but he leaned against her knees, saying that he was tired and had written no love-scene.

"Not with pen and ink, perhaps," replied his mother, "but there has been one written on your mind's tablets lately. Do not deny it! There is a certain look upon your face of which I am a connoisseur. Well, then, tell me of it! I would much rather hear it related than read."

Nadrovine moved his head as it lay against her arm, to signify that he had nothing either to read or to relate.

"Ah, bah! you are a stupid, sweet monster, like that fellow with the ass's head in the play. I am to be your Titania and tickle your ears as you sleep, I suppose? Now rise at once, and seat yourself opposite me, that I may look at you. But not on poor Scud!" she added, as Nadrovine prepared to throw himself into a low wicker chair in front of her. There was lying in it a dapper fox-terrier which she shook unceremoniously from the silk cushion upon the floor. "He is a nice little beast. I do not wish him out of the way, yet. And, besides, the proper

method will be to chloroform him, not to mash him
to a jelly."

" Why do you have a fox-terrier?" asked Nadrovine. " A Russian greyhound, or a deer-hound, or
even a Siberian blood-hound, would suit you far
better than that fidgety little *gommeux.*"

" Precisely why I like him, dear, great, but not
always discerning one! I dislike women who are
eternally posing for harmonious effects. I am naturally expected to own a sleuth-hound, or some monster of that sort, and to drive with my horses Russian fashion; therefore I prefer a fox-terrier and a
curricle with a pair of English bays harnessed in
the usual manner, as becomes a fading beauty with
more than five gray hairs visible in the most conspicuous waves of her tresses, and whose son writes
novels which add at least a hundred years to her
age."

She put one of her exquisite feet, in its silk
stocking and small embroidered *mule*, on the edge
of the chair in which he was sitting, and rubbed it
gently against him as she talked. She was nearly
head and shoulders taller than the Medici, but the
Medici could not have supported her plump body
upon those fine, delicately-modelled ankles.

Madame Nadrovine's wrists and ankles would
have been too small, had it not been for the perfect,
lithe symmetry of her whole superb figure. Her
white flesh was as hard and elastic as the flesh of a

young horse, and she had the eyes of a girl. Those eyes in the rich maturity of her face were like some flowers of spring blooming in the heart of summer. They were a girl's eyes, but experience spoke from every curve of the deeply-cut lips.

"'A fading beauty'!" echoed Nadrovine, clasping the narrow foot. "Small one! some one has been praising you lately, else you would not venture to say such a thing. And so you have five gray hairs? Give them to me, and I will have them made into a paint-brush to color that pretty mole on the left of your chin, there."

"*Le bon Dieu* has saved me that trouble, *mon cher*," replied his mother, tranquilly. "But your thought is a kindness, nevertheless. I will smoke now, I think. My cigarette-case, if you please." She extended her hand,—one of those beautiful hands whose palms look like crumpled pink tissue-paper, and yet which have the strength of machinery.

He handed her the simple silver case with its cipher—S. N.—in gold, and she snapped back the lid with an impatient click, finding it empty.

"I am rather glad of that," said Nadrovine, lazily reaching for papers and tobacco. "I enjoy nothing much more than seeing you roll cigarettes."

"Baby! I love you!" she replied, pressing him with a little movement of her foot. "By the way, Vladimir, have you your horse with you?"

"Czarina, you mean? Yes. Will you ride here?"

" Ride?" She paused to look at him, with the moist rose tip of her tongue against the cigarette which she was rolling. "Will I ride here? Dear great one! can you fancy me in any place two days, two hours, without being on horseback? If I am ever translated, I trust it will be in a saddle rather than a chariot."

" My horses are at your disposal, most dear."

She rose to light her cigarette over the lamp near which they were sitting. The light caught her curled eyelashes and the jut of her strongly-marked brows. He thought he detected a slight tremor at the corners of her mouth.

" Why do you smile?" he demanded, somewhat quickly.

" Oh, well,—at nothing,—at a thought." She pulled the fox-terrier's ears between her thumb and little finger, holding her cigarette in her first and third. Then, suddenly lifting her eyes upon his,—

" Am I ' most dear' ?"

Nadrovine started perceptibly. He felt his cheeks sting, and a certain bigness about his heart, which beat fiercely.

" Am I?" repeated his mother, serenely. She blew some rings of smoke from her rounded lips, and he thought with an absent-minded fancifulness that they looked like the ghosts of kisses.

" Why should you ask me such a question?" he inquired, finally, with abruptness.

"Why? Oh, because it suggested itself! I wondered. I put my wonder into words. There is the whole story."

"You will always be 'most dear' in your own peculiar way," said Nadrovine. He looked down at his left hand, surprised for the moment not to feel the familiar ring upon his finger. His mother followed his glance.

"In—my—own—peculiar—way?" she repeated, curiously. And then, "Your sapphire, my scribbler dear?—your unequalled 'Esto sol testis'? Where is he? Not lost?" There was again that little flicker at her mouth's edge.

"No, not lost," said Nadrovine.

"Well, and what then?"

"I took it off."

"You—took—it—off?" repeated his mother, with the same almost imperceptible pause between the words. She smiled openly this time. "And, pray, where did you put it?"

"Where it will be even safer," he answered, rallying suddenly. "Where the sun will be a better witness than ever."

"Oh! So!" said his mother.

"Come!" cried Nadrovine, rising to his feet. "It is so hot in here! Look at the poor moths on the table there, and your book curling in the lamp-light! Let us walk on the terrace. I know that you love the sea."

"Come, then," she replied. She stretched an arm out on either side, and let the end of her cigarette fall from her relaxed fingers. Her gown of cream-white Chinese silk hid the straining of her supple figure beneath its numerous folds. "Ah," she said, with clinched teeth, "that was a renewal of everything. Pull me up, and I can walk with you all night." He drew her to her feet, and they passed together into the hushed and radiant night without. A strong sea-air entered their nostrils, and lips parted to speak, changing the woman's mood and intensifying that of the man.

"One wishes one's self a star on a night like this!" she said, opening the folds of silk at her neck and expanding her splendid chest. "One wishes to be loved only by God and children!—one's own child," —she pressed upon the shoulder of her son,—"and the children of misfortune."

"My mother!" he said, forgetting, in that thrilled moment, even the eyes of Ilva.

"My son!" she returned. She stopped, hesitated, confronted him. "'For I, the Lord thy God, am a jealous God!'" she repeated. "Vladimir, that might read, 'For we, the women thy mothers, are jealous women!' To give up! It is impossible. It is impossible, Vladimir! To give up our own to strangers! To be forsaken! Our Lord has said that we must be forsaken. Yes! and God also said, 'Honor thy father and thy mother!' It is terrible! Why do those great words contradict each other? To give them up, our own, our heart's blood! —to give them up to little, pretty things who do not even know what it means to accept them,—to take them from us!"

She spoke to the sea, holding her strong throat with a hand on either side.

"To give them up, their eyes, their voices, their days, their nights, the talents and passions that they have drawn from our breasts. To give them up! —always to give them up! To be forsaken! To be content to be forsaken! To feel that we are second to what will forever be first with us! To remember our pain that gave them being, and to endure pain more frightful in resigning them! To know that they will never be wholly ours again! To know that their arms are only nests for others, their hearts quickened with another's image, their lips waiting for her, that heaven means only the possibility of her presence! Jealous? Jealous? Vladimir!"— her voice rang through him,—"where is your ring?"

X.

The sound of the sea seemed to cease for Nadrovine. He heard only the pumping of his quick blood past his ears. His mother's face shut out the phosphorescent line of surf beyond,—a face which was a shadow, broken only by the glittering questions of her eyes. He was dumb, overwhelmed by a vast distaste to sharing his secret even with her. He had not meant to reveal it for some days. Ilva, he knew, would remain silent until he told her to speak. His mother waited, moveless, wordless. He could hear her heart beating a little out of time with his,—more quickly and unevenly. She was still holding her throat in both hands, and her silk gown made a subdued, crisp noise in the varying wind which was not unlike an echo of the advancing, receding waves below.

He spoke at last, taking down her hands from her throat and placing them against his breast.

"Trust me, my mother!" he said. They were the first words that came to him.

"Show yourself worthy," she answered. "Let me trust you. Your ring, Vladimir!"

He stooped and kissed the hands that he held.

"If I tell you in a week, small one, will that do?"

"Why in a week?"

"It is a whim,—a desire. I beg of you, give me this week. Have you never wanted a week out of your life all to yourself, for no particular reason?"

"But why a week? Why not two weeks? Why not two days?"

"You will trust me?"

"I must!" She drew her hands impatiently away, —turned from him. The moon shone through the thin folds of her gown on either side, and her noble figure was dark between them.   Nadrovine followed her.

"You will do as I ask, little mother?"

"Why a week?" she reiterated, turning upon him.

He began to experience that sensation of hopeless exasperation which possesses one when questioned against one's will.

"I have said 'a week,'" he answered, controlling himself.   "It is a short time.   This is Tuesday night.   Next Tuesday night at this hour I will tell you."

"Perhaps I shall not care to know then," she said, harshly.   All softness had passed from her face. It was as expressionless as an inland lake when no wind is stirring.

"As you please," said Nadrovine.   He stood looking down at the sea, with his profile turned towards her.   The pain of being misunderstood was upon him, and that stripped feeling which accompanies any attempt of another, no matter how dear, to unveil our holy of holies.

"The sea is the water of youth," remarked his mother, turning abruptly, her voice light and unconcerned again.   "Paris is like Mr. Hyde, and the Riviera is like Dr. Jekyll, where one's health is concerned.   I feel much younger!"

They talked of his work and prospects, walking up and down in the moonlight until nearly one o'clock, when his mother left him to go to bed. She made no allusion to their first topic of conversation, but kissed him good-night on the cheek instead of on the lips.

If men realized how their mothers love them, there would be a new force in the world.

Nadrovine, on the contrary, thought his mother exacting and lacking in consideration for him.

He came upon her the next morning shortly after sunrise, with little Lotta Boutry at her side.

"An elf, Vladimir!" she called to him,—"a genuine elf! She is coming to breakfast with me. I have promised to have some woodbine for her to suck, and some candied violets for an *entrée*. She says she can fence,—with a bulrush, no doubt!"

"Oh, Signor Nadrovine," cried Lotta, "if this is your maman, I do not wonder you tell charming fairy-stories and that Cousine Ilva loves so to hear you talk! She is even more beautiful than you,— your maman, I mean,—and she speaks as charmingly!"

"Who is 'Cousine Ilva'?" said Madame Nadrovine.

"Your buttons are too much to the left, Mademoiselle Lotta," corrected Nadrovine. "Draw your right shoulder a trifle backward, I pray you."

"Cousine Ilva," said Mademoiselle Boutry,—"I thank you, Signor Nadrovine,—Cousine Ilva is the Signorina Demarini. She and Signor Nadrovine,

your son, are the greatest of friends. They take long
rides together,—long, long rides. And talk! Oh,
how they talk! One can hear them when one has
ridden far ahead,—a sort of murmur like a bee
caught in a flower,—um-um-um-um. Signor Nadrovine used to tell Cousine Ilva stories when she
was a little, *little* girl. He called her, ' doushka' then.
He was ' The Prince of the Silver Book,' I feel
convinced."

" Why?" said Madame Nadrovine.

" Because he calls her ' doushka.' "

" Oh! So he calls her ' doushka' now ?"

" Yes, madame."

" And what does she say in reply ?"

" She looks another way, or says nothing, or says,
' Signor ?' "

" You observe, do you not, *chérie ?*"

" I used to observe more than I do now, madame,
but maman has broken me of it somewhat. Whenever I look in the least solemn, she says, '*Qu'as-
tu, chérie ? As-tu de bo-bo ?*' Miss Herbert says that
means, in English, ' Art thou in the doomps?' "

" Thou hast not the ' doomps' this morning, then,
little one?" said Madame Nadrovine.

" Oh, no !" replied Lotta.

" And what did you say your cousine Ilva was
named ?"

" She is the Signorina Demarini."

" Demarini?" repeated Madame Nadrovine. She

knit her deeply-modelled brows. " Demarini? And your uncle, the Signor Demarini, what is he like?"

" I do not know him well. Fanny says that he has the nose of a shadow when one holds the candle in a wrong position."

" A Roman nose, then?"

" It has a hump, madame."

" How do you know, *petite?*"

" By his portrait in Aunt Anita's locket. But his hair, oh, it is lovely! Like astrachan. So black! so curly! One would not think of his nose again when one had looked at his hair."

" You are a delightful morsel," said Madame Nadrovine,—" as complete as a little mole on a pretty woman's cheek."

" You have two moles," said Lotta, composedly, " and of such a lovely brown. They are just like little bits of a negro's skin pasted upon yours. Maman had a little negro page one year. He stole so much sugar that it gave him some disease and he died. He was odious. I prayed not to be glad. But it was at Christmas. *Le bon Dieu* had so much to attend to that probably he did not listen to me."

" Why?" asked Madame Nadrovine for the second time.

" Oh, well, because," replied Mademoiselle Boutry,—" because I *was* glad. He used to bite pieces out of my wax dolls and chew them. He was very odious. One could not call one's dolls

one's own, when he was by. Little negroes are
hateful things. One night maman let me sit up to
see an eclipse of the moon. It came to me then.
Little negroes are like eclipses of the stars. We—
we white children are like real stars, and little
negroes are like eclipsed stars,—brown, dull and
horrid. Fancy a heaven of eclipsed stars, monsieur, with an eclipsed moon for maman! Bah!"
She galloped ahead a little way.

"I wish to chaperon her at her first ball, great
one," said Madame Nadrovine over her shoulder.

"You like arduous tasks," replied Nadrovine,
dryly.

"Arduous!" exclaimed his mother. "I should
like to drive a comet with its tail for reins—that is
all! Brilliant! The child is a fairy, with a diamond
for a mind. One could write on crystal with it."

"Or glass," said Nadrovine.

"Oh, yes, glass," repeated his mother,—"glass
made from the ashes of great men and the sands of
time."

"You will spoil her, small one."

"If I did not, men would. It is always better
for a woman to be spoiled by women than by men."

"But she is a child, not a woman."

"Children are born women in this nineteenth
century. You hear how she talks?"

"Yes; it makes one laugh and shudder at the
same time." ·

"To say the least, that is a novel sensation. One generally combines tears with shuddering,—not laughter. Here she comes back again."

Lotta approached them on her pony, her cheeks like the inner lips of conch-shells, her hair riotous in the sharp morning wind.

"Oh, madame!" she cried, "see what a droll thing I have found! A little shell! So fine! so pretty! And yet when one holds it in one's hand it puts out horrid claws into one's palm."

"Throw it away," advised Madame Nadrovine.

Lotta regarded it gravely. "Cousine Ilva says that there is a lesson in everything," she remarked. "I have decided already upon this queer creature. It is like the curé of our village. He is so smooth, so quiet on the outside,—his shell, you know,—and then as soon as one begins to listen, to really be interested, he puts out his claws and scratches one. He hints at one's friends, especially when they are sitting in the front row and have new gowns on. Marie Dinôt had a new cap one Sunday, and a blue gown that maman gave her, and he said some things—some horrid things—about head-dresses and fine apparel. Marie fairly squirmed. I really wished to spread my own gown over her, she looked so embarrassed; and really, you know, it was immaterial to me."

"You are a little Samaritan," remarked Madame Nadrovine.

"Oh, I should like to be!" said Lotta. "But it is beyond me. Numa Roumestan"—she patted the pony's flat and muscular neck—"will not carry double. I could not take any one on my horse and pour oil on him,—not possibly,—because Numa would kick so frightfully."

"But you would wish to?" suggested Madame Nadrovine.

"Oh, yes, with all my heart. I would ride away and get Cousine Ilva, and she would tell me what to do."

"How good this Cousine Ilva must be!"

"There is no one so good, nor so pretty."

"Not even I?" asked her new friend. Lotta reined in Numa, and shaded her eyes in order to observe her carefully.

"You are not pretty," she announced, finally. "You are like a great picture which has been painted many years. Young girls might make you look like a picture,—a little pale, you know; but you make them look just what they are,—only young girls. I say it so badly. One feels you, madame, and one sees them. Your hair is so beautiful, like purple-beech leaves, and your eyes are the color of the moss on which they fall when the wind loosens them. Your skin is like a white cloud. It makes one think to look at you. When one looks at my cousine Ilva, one wishes to know what *she* thinks."

"Your name should be ' Wonderful,'" said Madame Nadrovine. "You are the only child that I ever coveted."

"If one could have two mammas," replied Lotta, "I would pray for you to be my second one."

"And how old are you?" asked her friend.

"Nine," answered Lotta, adding, gravely, "But I feel as though I had lived much longer. Other children of nine seem very young to me."

"I should think so!" murmured Madame Nadrovine.

XI.

Lotta found herself seated at a light wicker table, facing her new and fascinating acquaintance, with a plate of great silverish-blue hot-house grapes before her, a gold knife and fork, and a glass of pale-yellow wine at her side.

"Must I drink this?" she inquired, simply.

"If you wish," replied Madame Nadrovine.

The child tasted it and set it down.

"It is wine, is it not?" she asked. "I like it."

"Yes; it is Tokay."

"Cousine Ilva does not like wine. That is something the color of her hair."

"Then she is very fair?"

"Oh, very! Her eyes are darker than these grapes, but her skin is like—like—— It is whiter than yours, madame."

"And she and my son are great friends?"

"Oh, great! They ride, read, walk. I will taste that wine again, if I may, madame."

"Certainly, *chérie*. It is very light, like sunbeams. It is good for you. Will you drink my health?"

The child lifted the delicate glass to her thin, curved red lips.

"May you grow more and more beautiful every year, *chère madame*," said she.

"And may you increase in wit and in the likeness of Voltaire!" returned Madame Nadrovine, bowing over her second glass.

"Who was Voltaire?" asked Lotta, pausing with a grape half pressed from its juicy sheath. "Was he the man who said, 'Il y a des fagots et des fagots'? Cousine Ilva says that Shakespeare said, 'There are men and men,' before Voltaire said that. It was in my last lesson."

"A sound lesson," said Madame Nadrovine.

"It was a very hard one to learn," replied the child.

"Ah, we all find it so," remarked her friend, smiling. "Will you have some more of my pretty wine?"

"Yes, thank you so much. It must be made of sunbeams: it makes me feel like dancing, as they do. It seems as if I had a thousand things to tell you and as if they ought all to be said at once. I do not know where to begin." She swallowed another mouthful of the Tokay.

"Begin where you wish," said Madame Nadrovine.

Lotta held out her little hands and looked at them earnestly. They seemed strangely alive,—to have an existence apart from hers. At the same time a joyous importance possessed her: she believed that the green-eyed lady opposite her would attach great meaning to whatever she said and was anxious to hear her speak. She nodded her little head wisely. "I will tell you something," she announced, in a low voice. "I have never told it, even in my prayers. It is about Signor Nadrovine."

"Indeed?" said his mother. She replenished the glass of Tokay, and then leaned on an indolent white elbow, waiting for the child to continue.

"Yes, it is about them both,—about Cousine Ilva and Signor Nadrovine. It is my belief, madame—— Did I spill that grape-juice on the cloth, madame? I trust not. I have been taught never to spill things. My little American governess taught me. She never spills anything. She is charming. Her eyes are of a dark brown, with little three-cornered lights in them. But I was not going to talk about her?" She stopped with a slightly dazed expression, and put this statement in the form of a question.

"It was about my son and your cousine Ilva, was it not, *chérie?*"

"Yes. Why doesn't Signor Nadrovine come to

breakfast? Does he never get hungry? Why did he leave us?"

"He wanted to ride longer, I suppose. But the great secret which you were going to confide to me, *petite?*"

"Oh!" said Lotta. She pushed the glass of Tokay a little from her, and regarded it seriously, screwing her small brows together. "Oh!" she said, again. "It is not exactly a secret. An idea. My idea, madame. Only an idea of mine. A silly idea, perhaps. I think they are in love, like Graciosa and Percinet in the fairy-tale. Aunt Anita is like the Duchess Grognon. My aunt Anita is Cousine Ilva's mother. She is an American too, but she left her beauty in America, she says, with her American name. It was Ann. She is Anita in Italy. She has a long black tooth in front. It is like one of the black keys on a piano-forte, the rest are so white. She says the nerve was killed. But she has a great many left. She says that *they* will kill *her*. They go to sleep when she is quiet and reads yellow books, but when I play with Zi-Zi and Nicoletta they wake up and begin to jump up and down. That is the time when Cousine Ilva takes me to the little hill, and when Signor Nadrovine comes, and we cut up apricots and have feasts and strangle Zi-Zi and Signor Nadrovine steals the hair. I saw him. He wound it around his finger. I believe Cousine Ilva saw him too. She didn't say anything. But her eyes

looked. You know people's eyes *do* look. His do,
—Signor Nadrovine's, I mean. They look at her
as if she were an apricot and they wished they had
teeth, so that they could eat her up. They do, indeed.
Indeed, indeed they do. Oh, madame, how I am
talking! My tongue seems to go of itself. I have
such a pleasant little aching in my elbows and knees.
I could ride right into the middle of the sea, and
I don't believe it would drown me. I believe it
would roll up on each side, as it did for the Israelites. That is the way Mees Herbert does her hair.
I have often thought the part looked like the path
through the Red Sea,—it *is* so red, *red,* you know,
and it is heaped up in such big waves on either side.
I imagine that the hair-pins are the Egyptians all
sunk out of sight in it. And the little steel points
in her comb are the good Israelites, that have gotten
safely over. Cousine Ilva says she loathes that comb.
She used to learn her multiplication-table by looking
at it, and she never *could* remember how many of
those little steel points there were. Sometimes I
wonder if any one ever called Mees Herbert
'doushka.' It would be almost like calling Saint
Cecilia 'Cici,' or Saint Pierre 'Pierrot,' would it
not? Oh, how I talk! Will you forgive me?
Will you give me just three more grapes? They
are like the three bears, only they haven't bears'
paws. I don't know why I said that. It doesn't
seem to have much sense. But then wise things

don't seem to have much sense. Those words cut
in the ring that Cousine Ilva wears around her neck,
—she showed them to me and explained them, but
they seemed not to have much meaning to me. Something about the sun. It was Latin. I don't think
the Latin people could have understood each other
very well. Perhaps they prayed in French, you
know, madame. I am sure God speaks French. It
would seem *so* unnatural for him to speak English,
or German. He must understand them all, of
course, but I am *sure* that he himself speaks in
French."

"And the words on the ring were Latin?"

"Cousine Ilva told me so. She kissed it. It
was an Italian kiss, no matter what the words are.
It seems silly to wear a ring on a ribbon. One
might as well wear one's shoe on one's hat. I beg
you to forgive me, madame. I really feel as if my
eyes and nose and ears would begin to talk presently.
I feel so happy, and yet I feel like weeping, too. I
seem to love you more than any one in the world,
and then that makes me wish to cry, because there
is Cousine Ilva, and maman, and my dear friend
Signor Nadrovine. I should have said your dear
son. Please think I meant your dear son, or merely
your son, whichever you prefer."

Again she lifted the wineglass to her lips. Madame
Nadrovine, still leaning on her elbow, watched her
lazily, a smile just lifting the corners of her round

lips. She used sometimes to catch dragon-flies by
their steel-blue wings and dip them in her wineglass
until they were quite intoxicated, watching their sub-
sequent efforts to fly, with just such a flitting smile.
They would whirr their wings helplessly for a second
or two, and then deliberately turn their long bodies
over their heads in a species of leisurely back sum-
mersault. She had the same sense of amusement
now in noting the actions and words of the child opposite her, after her fourth glass of Tokay : besides,
she was learning all that she wished to know, in the
easiest and most detailed manner.

"So she wears this ring on a ribbon around her
neck ?" she asked, finally. "What color is it,
chérie ?"

"The ring, or the ribbon?" demanded Lotta, as
solemnly as though affairs of state depended upon
the reply.

"The ring."

"The ring is blue,—a black-blue. The ribbon is
white. I asked her why she did not wear it on her
finger, and she said, 'Because.' That was only last
night. I slept with her. Nini pinched me, and I
went to Cousine Ilva's room in the middle of the
night, and she was sitting up reading her Bible in
her chemise, and I saw the ring around her throat.
I will have ten rings when I have a lover, one for
each finger, and they must be of ten different colors,
and I think I will have little bars of music cut on

them instead of words. Tra! la! la! Tra! la! la! Just fancy! I could hold up my hands and one could play a tune on the piano by looking at them. Oh, madame, why, why do I say such things? I am not so silly usually, nor impertinent. I talk too much, but not so much as I have to-day, and then I cannot stop. My mind seems to be running on a little track, with steam to push it. If I let it stop, it will run off the track and break, or so it seems to me. Do you know, madame, I believe my head is lined with that lovely yellow wine? I seem to see with the backs of my eyes as well as with the fronts of them, and my head is such a lovely pink inside, with a lining of that yellow wine. I feel as though I must come into your arms and put my head just there on that little crease in your bodice. I fancy that your heart is under it. I want you to love me, madame. I beg you to love me. I beg you to tell me that you love me. Oh, I shall be so unhappy, so desolated, if you do not say that you love me! And, madame,"—she held up a slender finger of warning, and fastened her swimming gray eyes on those of Nadrovine's mother,—"and, madame," she repeated, "you must mean it. I could not bear it if you did not mean it. It would be nothing to me. I would weep indeed. Oh, I feel as though there were a whole ocean behind my eyes waiting to turn into tears at the first cross word." She dropped her little, dark head on the table, nearly into her plate, and fenced it about with her small fingers. "Oh! oh!" she sobbed, "do not let any one be harsh to me! I could not bear it! I could not bear it! Oh, I do not mean to weep! Why, why is it? I do not cry easily. No one has been harsh to me; and I do so wish to be silent. Why is it that I talk on and on? Oh, if you would —only love me, madame!"

Madame Nadrovine rose, biting her lips, and drew the airy figure into her arms.

"There, there!" she said, soothingly. She adored children, and this one was peculiarly adorable. She pressed her very close, and nipped the little, moist cheek with her strong lips. "There, there!" she repeated, "I do love you. You are a little darling. I wish you were mine. You are the dearest little dark-light in all the world. Your hair is like a mass of sun-rays that have been turned black for shining on naughty things. Your little mouth would woo a woman from thoughts of her lover. You are a little love, love, love," she crooned, rocking the distressed elf caressingly and singing the words to a minor air. "My little love, love, love. And I love you with all my heart. There, now, go to sleep. There, now, go to sleep. Go to sleep." She rocked her back and forth unceasingly, chanting the word "sleep" in various keys, until the child was actually sleeping on her breast. Then she loosened her arms, and looked down at the slight relaxed figure in its

i

pearl-gray riding-habit, stretched limply across her knees. She lifted one of the little half-curled hands and kissed its pale-rose palm twice, with soft, long kisses. The child's hair was damp, and matted upon her forehead. Madame Nadrovine lifted it, and fanned the warm brow with a crumpled napkin. Lotta slept on undisturbed. Her relaxed lips formed a piteous arch, her slightly-marked, delicate brows twitched uneasily with her dreams. She moved abruptly now and then, and tossed her slender limbs about.

Madame Nadrovine smiled again, shook her head, and drew the parted lips together in a really tender kiss.

"May you never be intoxicated with anything more dangerous than Tokay, you witchling!" she muttered.

Nadrovine entered, and found her bending over the child, who still slept heavily. He came towards them, looking anxious.

"Asleep?" he said. "What is wrong? Asleep at this time in the morning? I fear she isn't well. She looks like a delicate little thing."

"A little body and a great deal of soul," answered his mother, smiling again. "But she may have exhausted herself. She insisted on keeping up with me in all my gallops."

"No doubt that is it," assented Nadrovine. "But she is as white as her collar. What will you do with her?"

"I shall order a trap of some kind and drive with her at once to the Villa Demarini," she replied, serenely.

Nadrovine stooped to pick up her napkin, which had fallen near his feet.

"I will drive you," he said.

"But do not look so worried, Vladimir. She is only tired, I am sure. An hour's nap will refresh her absolutely. You see how quietly she sleeps?"

"Is it natural for sleeping children to be so pale?"

"Sometimes."

"Well, no doubt you know much better than I, but I will confess that I don't like that ghastly pallor. A trap will be at the door in ten minutes."

He left the room, and his mother sat silently, still rocking the sleeping child, and smiling to herself from time to time, with her eyes on the sea beyond.

XII.

Madame Nadrovine got into the phaeton without changing her habit, still holding Lotta in her arms. She tilted the child's hat above her face, in order to prevent the white morning light from disturbing her. Nadrovine drove the little chestnut cobs in silence, wondering less regarding this whim of his mother's than as to how much Lotta had revealed to her. The sea had that air of freshness which convinces one that it has just been created,—a long sparkle of cold blue against a belt of fawn-brown sand, like

a band of sapphires against the skin of a mulatto.
One felt the unsunned wind between one's eyelids
in a cool kiss, sweet with opening flowers as the hair
of a woman moist with sleep. The moon floated
overhead, a shred of light on the dark cobalt of the
sky.   There were clouds near the horizon, small
puffs of silver-white and green-gray.   This cool,
trembling morning, however, signified a hot noon.
It was as full of the promise of mid-day as a girl's
kiss of the passion of womanhood.   One knew that
four hours later the moon would have melted from
sight, that the sea would plunge heavily in waves
as of oil, that the crisp wind would sink to a sultry
sigh along the hot, steaming sands, and that to look
at the copper dome of the sky would cause one about
as much pleasure as to write an ode to the Queen of
the Salamanders on an August afternoon in Tangiers.

In the Villa Demarini no one seemed awake.
There was a gardener's boy training the geraniums
on one of the terraces, and a black caniche seriously
regarding the sea with ears erect. He was so absorbed in his contemplation that he did not even
bark as the phaeton drove up.

The gardener's boy, however, dropped his shears,
and came somewhat sheepishly to hold the horses
while Nadrovine got down and extended his arms
for Lotta.

" But what is one to do ?" asked his mother, making
no movement to resign the child to him, and looking

up at the closed blinds. "One can't leave the poor mouse on the veranda, and yet one doesn't wish to rouse the whole house."

The gardener's boy touched his hat.

"Gracious madam," said he, with a glutinous German accent, "the young gentlemen are awake, but they are hiding for fear that the young lady is killed. They stopped to talk to some boys on the shore, and the Fräulein galloped away. They thought that perhaps she was drowned. The Fräulein Ilva was bathing, and I told her. She rode off on Herr Georges's pony. She has been gone half an hour. No one else is awake. The Fräulein and her brothers ride always alone at this hour in the morning."

"In what direction did the Signorina Ilva go?" asked Nadrovine, quickly.

"Towards the village, mein Herr. Shall I awaken the nurse-maid?"

"Suppose we drive towards the village and try to meet her?" suggested Nadrovine to his mother. "She must have turned back by this time."

Just at this moment the short strokes of a pony's legs sounded on the gravel, and Ilva approached them, her gown of pale-blue gingham modelled damply to her shoulders and arms, her thick hair uncoiling at her throat, hatless, gloveless, even shoeless, in her haste. She was paler than Lotta, and her lips quivered. Nadrovine lifted her from the pony without even greeting her, and assisted her into the phaeton beside his mother. She could not speak, but put her hand on Lotta's little body and began to draw deep breaths, the color running gradually back into lips and cheeks.

"I am afraid you have been sadly frightened," said Madame Nadrovine, at last. "It was very thoughtless of me to keep the child, but she fascinated me so that I was scarcely responsible. She is a perfect little Rosalind with a Titania's body, and of such a charming order of beauty."

"This is my mother, signorina," said Nadrovine.

"I—I—thank you!" replied the girl, and then blushed intensely. "I mean, I am most happy to know you, madame! Signor Nadrovine has spoken much about you. Will you tell me how you found her? Was she thrown? Is she unconscious, or only asleep? Her mother worships her so. It would have killed her."

"Oh, I think she is merely exhausted," answered Madame Nadrovine. "If she could be undressed without waking her——"

"What is all this?" cried a voice behind them. "Has anything happened to the child?" A tall figure approached,—the figure of a man with closely-curling dark hair, soaked from his sea-bath, a large, aquiline nose finely cut, clear lips, pale but handsome, and the complexion of a seckel pear.

"Madame Nadrovine!" he exclaimed.

"Myself, count," she replied, bowing slightly. Her eyes wore an amused expression above her grave mouth.

"Dear papa," said Ilva, "will you lift Lotta out and carry her up-stairs? I would like to put her to bed before Aunt Cecilia wakes."

Her father held out his arms mechanically, and Madame Nadrovine lifted Lotta's little limp form upon them.

"Do not jar her, count," she enjoined. There were veiled sparkles of mischief in her verdant eyes as she watched him ascend the steps of the veranda with the sleeping child in his arms.

"Will you not have a glass of wine, madame?" asked Ilva, somewhat nervously, as her father disappeared. She was painfully conscious of her dishevelled appearance in contrast with the complete attire of the woman in the black habit and top-hat. She felt that those eyes, with their jade-colored high lights, were taking her in from head to foot, and that her damp gingham gown was attracting their criticism.

"I will get you a glass of wine myself," she repeated, vaguely.

Madame Nadrovine made a gesture of negation with her handsome, ungloved hand.

"Thanks!" she replied. "I have had my grapes and coffee, and also a glass of Tokay. I fear we are detaining you, mademoiselle. We will call again to ask after the little Lotta."

"You will have nothing?" asked Ilva, disappointed in spite of herself. "It will not take a moment. My aunt will wish to thank you."

"Nothing will afford me more pleasure than to give her another opportunity," rejoined Madame Nadrovine, graciously. She made a few more amiable remarks, and was driven off by her son just as Count Demarini appeared on the veranda, having consigned Lotta to her nurse.

"This afternoon," Nadrovine had whispered to Ilva as he passed her to get into the phaeton. Her heart was throbbing with emotions as contradictory as strange, when her father ran hurriedly down the steps and put his hand on her shoulder.

"How long have you known Madame Nadrovine?" he asked, abruptly.

Ilva lifted to him her frankly surprised eyes.

"What a coincidence that you should know her so well, papa!" she said. "I have met her this morning for the first time. How beautiful she is! It is almost unearthly. Her eyes are like a Lorelei's, so green and liquid,—just the tint in a hollowing wave. Where did you know her, papa?"

"She has been the beauty of Paris for two seasons. Is she to be here long? I thought her in Hombourg."

"She is to spend the summer with Signor Nadrovine, her son. How absurd, papa, that she should have a son as old as that! She looks like his elder sister. What strange, strange eyes! All the green lights of heaven and earth seem to shine in them alternately,—the light of water, of grass, of glow-worms, of stars, of lightning, of peacocks' breasts, of precious stones. But, dear papa, I have not said 'how do you do?' to you. I sat up very late last night to welcome you, but they said that the train was three hours late, and so I went to bed. Have you been here long?"

"An hour,—two hours, perhaps. What is the matter with the child?"

"With Lotta?"

"Yes."

"I do not know. Nothing serious, I am sure. Madame Nadrovine said that it was probably exhaustion."

She was rather in awe of her father, but took his hand and kissed it shyly, while he stood silent, pulling the ears of the caniche, who was fawning upon him with wriggling body and lapping tongue.

He smiled absently and stroked her cheek and throat. He was proud of her beauty and talents, but utterly unfamiliar with herself. She was a school-girl still, and he might as well have tried to take interest in an expurgated edition of the poets.

"Dear papa, it seems so long since I have seen you!" she said, in a low voice. She pressed timidly against him, feeling the need of parental love to complete the love of the lover. Her mother was the last person in the world from whom she would have sought sympathy, either openly or surreptitiously, but her father, though seldom at home, and rarely noticing her, was always amiable on those occasions when he did condescend to pay her some little attention. As for the girl, she loved him with that blind and idealized affection which imaginative people sometimes bestow on those whom custom bids them revere, regardless of circumstances. His slight caress thrilled her very heart's core, and she longed to hide her face on his knees and tell him of her love for Nadrovine and ask his approval. She was frightened at the wonderful reality which life had suddenly assumed. All her past seemed receding, like a chaos of dreams from which one has been roused by a fall. She longed for some one to assure her that other women had given themselves, their ambitions, their ideas, their hopes, as utterly as she had done.

"You love me, papa?" she said, impulsively, looking down at his hand which she still held, that he might not see the tears which blurred her eyes. He started. A tear had fallen on his hand. Ilva wiped it hurriedly away with one of her own.

"Love you, my little Silverhair? Why, of course! Why are you crying? Is Miss Herbert harsh? I must speak to her."

"No, no, papa," said the girl.

"Then what is it? Why do you cry?" His

voice had an impatient ring, which she detected instantly in spite of her agitation.

"Lotta! it was Lotta!" she hastened to assure him. "I was so alarmed about her. I wondered if you or—or mamma would be so much grieved if I were to be hurt,—to die, perhaps. Oh, papa, do not notice me! I am very silly. I am thoroughly unnerved. I expected to come across the poor little thing lying dead at every corner that I turned."

"Poor little cat!" said her father, fondling her shoulder. "Too bad! too bad! I must speak to Cecilia about letting the children ride alone. There, now! go and change your clothes, my dear, and lie down. Have you a book to read? There is Feuillet's 'Roman d'un jeune Homme pauvre;' you are old enough to read that, I should think. It has an excellent moral. It ought to be in the library, on the second shelf of the bookcase, near the door. Or 'I Promessi Sposi;' you might read that. Tell your mother that you have my permission."

"Thank you," said the girl, biting her lips to repress a smile. Evidently her father did not know that since she could first read she might have perused every book in the house without fear of interruption. "Thank you, papa," she repeated, and began to walk slowly away in the direction of the house. They had been standing near the edge of the terrace.

Count Demarini called on Madame Nadrovine

that afternoon, to take her the heart-felt thanks of
Lotta's mother and his wife, who were both too
much overcome by the child's still somnolent inclinations to appear in person.   They were afraid of sunstroke, and sat all day fanning the slumberer, one on
each side of her little bed, with expressions of controlled apprehension.

Madame Nadrovine was alone when the footman
announced Demarini, teaching Scud to sing, by
striking dismal chords on a mandolin and pulling
his ear to accentuate the torture.

"How is the poor little one?" she said, placing
the mandolin on the floor at her side, and resuming
her rings, which she had taken off to facilitate the
singing-lesson.

Demarini seated himself opposite her, fondling
the fox-terrier's head much as he had fondled that
of his daughter during the past morning.   He kept
his eyes on Madame Nadrovine's hands, while she
kept hers upon his downcast lids.

"They fear a sunstroke," he replied.

"Ah! bah!" shrugged she, "what a thing it is
to have children! What cowards they make of one!
The child was worn out."

"Yes, probably," assented Demarini.   He returned her compelling gaze presently.

"I thought you were in Hombourg?" he said,
under his breath.

She lifted her brows until there were two or three

fine wrinkles in her smooth forehead, tuning the mandolin meanwhile to another key.

"And so I was. What would you have? One can't stay in one place forever?"

"One could," said Demarini, uncertainly, "if one were permitted," he added, in a low voice.

"One could do numberless things if one were permitted," replied Madame Nadrovine.

Again Demarini looked at her,—a flashing look. It lit up his swarthy face like the gleam from an almost extinguished fire on the ceiling of a dark room.

"Do you think I knew you were here?" he asked.

"I? Oh, it is much too warm to think. Besides, coincidences fill up every inexplicable gap in life."

"You know that I would not have come when it was not your wish. I would not have called this afternoon save to explain my presence in your neighborhood."

She made him a little bow, full of mockery and a teasing amusement.

"I am in your debt, monsieur."

He half started to his feet.

"You are not angry? You do not bid me go, Sereda?"

"Pardon me, count, I took a slight cold in sleeping near an open window on my way from Hombourg. It has made me a little deaf. Will you have the kindness to repeat that last sentence?"

He stood before her, grasping his hat in both hands, the veins in his temples swelling.

"You know that I love you to madness," he said, controlling himself. "I have called you by your name before. You know that I had rather be laughed at by you than caressed by any other. You own me absolutely, body and soul."

"And you own a charming daughter. She is like a young Psyche, a Psyche who will néver make the mistake of dropping hot oil on her Cupid. She will peep at him by moonlight or the reflection of a star in a mirror. But that damp blue cotton gown was as charming on her pretty bust as a peplos."

"Do you tell me to go?"

"My dear Demarini, if I told you to go you would assuredly stay."

"I would do what you told me."

"Do what you wish, I pray you."

"You are ungenerous."

"I have tried to overcome that fault in vain."

"You torture me?"

"Your endurance is that of a hero."

"You know that I only live for your pleasure."

"I fear that your sacrifice is vain."

"Sereda!"

"I beg of you, monsieur. My name is not ugly enough to be picturesque. There is an English rhyme that I remember:

> " ' Call me Daphne, call me Chloris,
> Call me Lalage or Doris.'

There are four names to choose from. Any substitute will do."

Demarini missed an excellent opportunity by his lack of knowledge. With what an air he could have finished the quotation, "Only, only call me thine !"

Madame Nadrovine had taken an unfair advantage of his ignorance of English.

He could only repeat himself passionately:

"But you do not tell me to go? You do not tell me to leave Italy? *Oh! que je suis fou! Que je vous adore! Que je vous adore!*"

He caught the loose sleeve of her gown and pressed it against his lips.

"It is not yet paid for," she laughed, regarding him lazily. "It is the property of Félix that you are caressing."

"You wear it : that is sufficient. Why do you always mock me?"

"That I may not be mocked myself."

"You do not hate me?"

"I have not capacity for so extreme an exertion."

"And I may call upon you?"

"If you will take the chance of finding me out when you call."

"It is enough to live under the same constellations that shine above you."

" And what when it is cloudy?"

" It is better to share clouds with you than sunshine with another."

" You deserve something for that speech."

" What? what, Sereda?"

" A kind message to take back in regard to the little Lotta. Say that I will call to-morrow afternoon to drive her in my phaeton. And now I must pray you to excuse me," she concluded, looking at a little watch which hung from a thread-like bracelet on her left arm. " I have only three-quarters of an hour in which to make my toilet for dinner. Say to the little one that I love her dearly and await our next interview with impatience."

She took a cigarette from her case, after extending it to Demarini, who extracted one eagerly with trembling fingers, and lighted it unconcernedly as he left the room. He saw her slightly smiling face, with its placid, downcast lids, in the pale light of the fuse, as he glanced back at her before letting the folds of the portière fall between them. Scud had jumped up in her lap, and was lapping her smooth chin with his thin pink tongue.

" The little beast!" said Demarini, shutting his teeth hard on the last word. He had the aversion of most men to seeing a pet dog in contact with a woman, and when that woman was the object of the sincerest folly of his life it became insupportable. He would have wrung the dog's neck without the slightest compunction, could he have been sure of remaining undiscovered.

XIII.

No sooner had Demarini left the house than Madame Nadrovine's whole aspect changed entirely. She threw the just-lighted cigarette from her, and watched it smoke of itself on the red tiles of the floor, holding either arm of her chair and caressing her under lip with her tongue, in absolute absorption. Scud touched the half-extinguished cigarette with his inquisitive black nose, and sprang back uttering a short howl of pain, to seek protection in the skirts of his mistress. She stroked his dapper little head absently, her great eyes fixed on the floor a yard or two beyond.

"I have it, Scud!" she exclaimed, finally. "It is as clear as your eyes, my beauty!" She hugged him in the nook of her arm as though he had been a child, and he cuddled up to her, making little wet noises of pleasure with his flexible tongue.

"We shall see what he will have to tell me next Tuesday, little sleek one! Now kiss my ear because I have confided in you, *petit !*"

Scud saluted the salmon-pink ear turned to him, with rapturous iteration. He looked into her face precisely as if he understood everything, and then pushed a soft paw into her cheek as a baby pushes its soft hand. He was an exceedingly human little

G   k   13

beast.   Madame Nadrovine felt as though she had
really confided her plan to an approving friend.   She
kissed the little dog twice on the top of his smooth
head, and then put him down from her lap.

The next day she called again at the Villa Demarini, to inquire after Mademoiselle Boutry.   Ilva
was the first to enter the drawing-room.   She had
on a Roman shirt, and her bare throat rose charmingly from its loose folds.   Madame Nadrovine
noted the extreme beauty of her slight hands and
wrists.   Her blond hair was arranged loosely in a
strange coiffure: one could not tell where it began
or ended.   It looked as though her head were cased
in a helmet of silverish gold.   "Lotta seems quite
herself to-day," she said, adding, half awkwardly,
"She seems also in love with you, madame."

"I fear, then, that she is fickle, mademoiselle,"
smiled Nadrovine's mother.   "Yesterday she was
your ardent slave."

"Sensitive children are always won by beauty,"
replied Ilva, and then flushed, feeling that she had
said something bluntly flattering.

"How *gauche!* how utterly unsophisticated!" said
Madame Nadrovine to herself.   "But she has a
wonderful profile,—like those on old coins.   And
what a figure!—the hips of a girl and the breast
of a goddess!"

Ilva, wishing to appear at her best, naturally appeared at her worst.   Madame Nadrovine left, won-

dering what Vladimir saw in the child beyond that beauty of youth which the adored and the adorer so soon outgrow.

She called to Nadrovine that evening as he was returning with the pressure of the girl's lips yet pulsing upon his.

He approached slowly. She was pulling the dried leaves from some heliotrope-plants, her purplish-black hair falling in a heavy plait far below her waist. Some of the violet heliotrope-branches were thrust through the girdle of yellow brocade.

"I called at the Villa Demarini this morning, Vladimir," she said, without pausing in her occupation. "The little one has quite recovered. And I saw that pretty young girl again. She is as adorably lovely as she is deplorably silly."

"Silly, small one?" asked Nadrovine, with a smile whose complaisance goaded his mother to a frown. "In what did her silliness consist?"

"Oh, as for that, I do not recall exactly. It was the general impression. But, of course, if she is not silly in your eyes I accept your judgment, you have known her so much longer than I have."

"Since she was a child of ten," replied Nadrovine.

"Indeed?" said his mother. She drew down a yellow rose which drooped from a trellis overhead, and began stripping it of its blighted outer leaves. "It is strange what opposite impressions different people make on different people."

" Yes ; I have thought that," admitted Nadrovine.

His mother changed the conversation with her usual unfailing tact. An hour later they were dining alone together, the last flush of sunset striking across the silver and glass of the dinner-table and firing Madame Nadrovine's thick hair.

" I suppose you have heard of Neivensky's marriage?" she said, holding her interlaced hands about her small claret-glass. "Of course it will be the end of his career."

" Why?" asked Nadrovine. He was thinking of that last look in Ilva's eyes,—a look of intense love and pleading. "I fear your mother does not like me. Try to make her like me," she had said to him. She had held him from her except for that last kiss. "I feel that she would not wish it," she had whispered. And she had agreed with him that it was best not to tell either his mother or her own until a week had passed.

" It would be so much to happen all at once. I will be so thankful to have my heart beat quietly for a little while." Those were her words at parting. He had not touched her, except to take from her that one kiss, not yet the kiss of a lover,—she lifted her lips so frankly. He could not bear to rouse her from her ethereal dreams. She would only love him more when she comprehended.

" Why?" he repeated.

" Oh, it goes without saying," answered his mother.

"She is a little country-girl,—as lovely as one's dream of a cool brook in summer, but so ignorant of everything, even of love, which she undoubtedly possesses in great quantities."

"You have seen her, then?" said Nadrovine.

"Twice. Her eyes were glued on him, and she spoke to óne without turning her head. If there could be as many babies as disillusions during the next six years, perhaps they might be happy."

"Do you think the only hope of married people lies in their offspring?"

"In those cases where men of genius marry commonplace women, I do, most assuredly."

"And what when men of genius marry women of genius?"

"One might as well say, 'How if man's inclinations and Heaven's decrees ran in the same direction?' or, 'What if love were ever given by two people in like proportion?' I must say, Vladimir, that outside of your novels your remarks are the reverse of sagacious. If men of genius were to marry women of genius, the story of the garden of Eden would sink into insignificance, and one would accept the grave cheerfully as the consummation of such an existence, smiling at the idea of a heaven where there is no marriage nor giving in marriage."

"But you believe in the marriage of true minds?" ventured her son.

"It is a union as vague as that of Saint Cecilia

and her heavenly lover,—who, by the way, permitted her to be beheaded! After all, those celestial unions invariably end by one of the participants losing their heads: do you not think so?" She smiled provokingly with her long eyes, and reached for a bunch of grapes, holding back her sleeve with one supple hand.

"I think it depends," said Nadrovine, beginning to realize that the task of breaking his engagement to his mother would not be an easy one. "It depends upon the people," he continued; "and also upon what one considers a 'celestial union.'"

"Oh, that is easy enough to explain!" exclaimed Madame Nadrovine. "It is where souls are chiefly mentioned and bodies are regarded as mere accidents; where love-looks are more than kisses, and words than hand-pressures. These are the wings of love. Lovers amuse themselves in pulling them off, as little boys find occupation in maiming flies. When this is accomplished and love is left crawling, they forget that it once had wings, and speak of it as though it had been always the mere grub that it now appears."

"That is not your real idea of love, I am sure, small one," said Nadrovine, with a sudden grip of revulsion which he conquered at once. "Pure love sanctifies the body which it inhabits. And its wings grow stronger with each effort to fly,—like the wings of a young bird. A true man cherishes each feather of the wings of love, instead of attempting to pluck them out. You have some reason for wishing to tease me : is it not so ?"

His mother lifted her brows slightly without looking at him. " It is true, then, that you believe what you say in your books regarding love ?"

" Why should you think otherwise ?"

" Merely because you have lived nine-and-twenty years in the world, and that most people who have lived that length of time have seen it that it is not good."

" There may be good love in a bad world, may there not, dear small one ?"

" There would be more probability of bad love in a good world." She stopped in her reckless speech, noting his chilled expression, to rise and droop over him with her exquisite grace of motherhood.

" How seriously you take my frivolous chatter, dear great one !" she said, letting her lips move against his cheek in forming these words. " Of course there is good love,—the love of all mothers for their children,—my love for you !"

This short conversation served to show her how completely in earnest he was. There was that seriousness of speech and manner which only accompanies a great and sincere passion. There would not be the slightest use in arguing with him : of that she was convinced absolutely and at once. Any frustration of what she chose to consider this disastrous affair must depend upon her, and upon her alone. She was quite determined, and the next time that Demarini called he found her in. She laughed at him, it is true, and lashed him unmercifully with her steely wit, but she did not forbid him to repeat his visit, and she consented to ride with him on the following afternoon. They met her son, his daughter, and Lotta on their way home.

"How lovely, how lovely your mother is!" sighed the girl. "But something tells me that she will never like me."

"She has only to know you," said Nadrovine.

"But it will be so hard for me to let her know me, feeling that she has an antipathy for me."

Nadrovine smiled with the perfect confidence of a man thoroughly in love regarding his lady's powers of charming.

"You smile because you think that I am exaggerating," said Ilva ; "but I feel such an absolute conviction that it is more serious than you think."

They were walking down the old rose-garden towards the sea. She had changed her habit for a gown of thin, soft, white stuff which fell in supple plaits close to her slight limbs. There was an old-silver girdle about her waist, and she had pulled a branch of blush-roses diagonally through it. The pink flowers were reflected faintly in the dull silver. A band of the same metal held her elastic hair in place, but it was loosened above her eyes, which were the color of. the sea at twilight, under her clear brows. Lotta was some way in front of them, absorbed in her dolls and Gaulois the caniche.

"I feel that it is serious," said Ilva, raising her eyes to his. "I feel that I can never make her like me."

"But, doushka, you have seen her how many times?—once, is it not?"

"And, oh! I was so embarrassed, I could think of nothing. I stammered, I said everything wrong. She must have thought me quite a little fool; and I could see even in that short time that to be foolish was the worst of all in her eyes. Generally I am so calm. I have never known what it is to feel ill at ease."

"You were too anxious, my princess."

"Yes, perhaps that was it. But I have spoiled everything."

"You have spoiled me," smiled Nadrovine.

"In what way? What do you mean?"

"Why, all faces are so meaningless to me since I have seen yours. The world is so empty where you are not. It makes my heart beat just to think of your eyes, and to remember your lips——"

He drew her to him by her slight wrists.

"Dear heart, why do you tremble?"

"You are trembling too," she whispered.

"It is because I love you so much."

"And I——"

"Divide my love by all the stars of Italy, and perhaps yours will be half of that."

"Multiply your love by every snow-flake that has ever fallen in Russia, and perhaps it will equal one-tenth of mine."·

He released her wrists and took her gently but strongly into his arms. Her lovely blond head leaned back against his breast, her lips were parted, her eyes fastened upon his. A sweet, intense pallor swept her face from brow to chin. She felt the deep throbbing of his heart beneath her cheek.

"Ilva," he said, "I have never kissed you as a man kisses the woman whom he loves above all others, and who has promised to become his wife. Will you let me give you that kiss of kisses? It will make you mine forever. No ceremony, no words of man, could seal you to me more entirely, my little one, my poet, my wife. Will you give me your lips as a sign that you have given me your heart and your soul?"

She did not answer him, but neither did she attempt to draw away. He felt the slight, quivering arms press him a little closer, and then he bent his face upon hers. She sank down· weeping from that controlled yet masterful caress, the tears of a young girl who feels that she has given her past and future irrevocably into the hands of another, and who knows that she can never be entirely her own again, in this world or in any world above.

"I love you, I love you," was all that Nadrovine could win from her in reply to his entreaties and self-reproaches. "No, no! you have done nothing. You have not wounded me. I—I love you more than ever. But there is something gone,—something that can never be the same. We can never live over the last half-hour again. Oh, how awkwardly I say it! I feel the same, and yet different. It is like these roses in my belt. They are roses, but their stems have been broken; they have been gathered." She cried softly, hiding her face in her hands and leaning it against his breast.

"My rose, whom I will wear forever," he whispered, pressing the small head against him. When she looked up at last, he drew the sign of the cross in her own tears upon her lips.

"They are doubly mine now," he said, with the smile which she thought like light. She reached up, drew down his head, and kissed him of her own accord, timidly, upon both eyes.

It was Tuesday afternoon.

XIV.

On his way home, Nadrovine recalled the fact that he had promised to reveal to his mother this night the history of his missing ring. The recollected clasp of Ilva's arms about his body seemed to give him strength, and he determined to announce his engagement as soon as he entered his mother's boudoir.

He ran up the shallow steps easily, noiselessly, smiling
to himself. He imagined the scene that would follow
his disclosure; but it was almost pleasant to think
of enduring even such pangs for the sake of his
lady. He lifted the portière softly and paused on
the threshold, seeing that Count Demarini was seated
near his mother, talking earnestly. No doubt they
were speaking on the very subject which he had
intended to broach. He hesitated. For an instant
her eyes seemed to rest on him, but he felt that he
was mistaken, for she returned at once to her conversation with Count Demarini, more absorbedly
than before. She had a great nosegay of roses and
heliotrope in her hand, and laughed as she pressed
them against Demarini's nostrils, hiding his whole
face. Her gown, of a curious dull-green silk, had
gold threads through it, which caught the light.
Her black hair made a shadowy haze about the
rich pallor of her face. Nadrovine was pierced by
her beauty and the luxurious grace of her sidelong
posture.

He saw Demarini seize the wrist of the hand which
held the bunch of roses, tear the roses from it, and
dash them upon the floor, at the same time drawing
her down into his arms. She rested against him,
her lips upon his. It was a long, silent kiss.

Nadrovine loosened the portière, and it resumed
its heavy folds without a sound.

"It must be nearly eight o'clock. Time to dress

for dinner," he said, aloud. He took out his watch
and looked at it, walking slowly along the cool hall
to the room where he usually smoked. There were
no candles lighted yet, and the afternoon glow fell
dimly through the swaying white curtains. He went
and leaned against one of the arched windows.

The individuality of inanimate objects began to
impress him,—the indifference of the sea, the self-
satisfaction of white sails moving placidly further
and further towards the citrine west. A branch of
small white flowers near him seemed vain of their
beauty, in their tremulous tossings back and forth.
There was an impassive stolidity about earth and
sky which irritated him. He heard two servants
laughing in the shrubbery on one side, and felt that
they had been wilfully impertinent. Twilight descended gradually, like the ceasing of a dream. The
sky was alternately a faded blue, a deep indigo, a
black-violet in which the gathering stars vibrated
glow-worm green, yellow of tigers' eyes, red of
cactus-flowers, the silver of frost in moonlight.

He stood there until darkness had formed densely
over land and water, and a servant entered bringing
candles. "Take them away," he said. Gloom again
surrounded him. He was thinking of his childhood,
—recalling the folk-lore in which his mother was so
learned, and which she used to repeat to him in her
charming voice; the quaint airs which she used to
sing to him, and in which he fancied he heard the

barking of wolves, the breaking of horses' feet through the crust of the snow, the cry of the child tossed out as a sacrifice for the others in the quickly-gliding sleigh. He saw his mother upon his father's knee, her black hair mingling with his red-brown beard. Her emerald ring had caught in it one day as she patted his cheek, and he had pretended to weep. She had also pretended to count the tears, and had given him a kiss for each. Then he was a boy, with her breath on his throat as she leaned to help him with his Virgil. Her rich voice had made the flexible verse throb like bars of music. He had been so proud of her. None of his playmates had possessed mothers who could help them with their Virgils. She had risen from a bed of illness to be present at his first communion. He could feel her tremble as she folded him afterwards in her arms and set her lips upon his head. She had sat on the edge of his little iron bed nearly all that night, and then they had prayed together until it was morning. He remembered her kindly smiles and praises of his first interlined manuscript,—her astonished commendation of the one which he brought her a year later,—the pride which broke through her eyes, like light through a forming wave, when he put his first printed book into her hands. She had kissed his hair, his eyes, his lips.

"My mother! my mother! my mother!" he whispered, between hoarse sobs, sinking down and taking

his head between his locked arms. Then he rose
to his feet, passing quickly from the house, and leaning on the old stone gate of the garden, still with his
eyes on the sea, in which the stars seemed to collect
and scatter like drops of quicksilver. There were
footsteps shortly, and a man's voice humming an air
from "Faust." Nadrovine stepped quietly into the
gravelled path before him, and Demarini stopped,
hesitating. He did not recognize the figure that confronted him.

"My friends will wait on you to-morrow," said
Nadrovine. "A quarrel at cards."

"Ebbene, signor," replied the Italian. He passed
on with a perfect comprehension of what had happened, but considered that kiss well bought. He
resumed the air from "Faust," and Nadrovine heard
it ringing out clearly on the tense quiet of the night.

He returned to the house.

"Vladimir?" said his mother, who had come to
meet him. She spoke uncertainly, and this went to
his heart. He had not yet realized the enormity of
it all.

"Vladimir, are you there?" she repeated. He did
not speak, but made a movement of assent. They
stood facing each other, and the slender curve of the
rising moon shed a strange light between them.

"Are you there?" she said again. "What is the
matter? Why don't you answer me?"

He moved back as she advanced towards him. "I

know,—I have seen—— No, no," he said, as she attempted to put her hand on his arm. He tried to continue. "I was going to tell you. I went to your boudoir. I meant to tell you——" He stopped again, shuddering violently.

"You meant to tell me what?" said his mother.

There was an absolute silence for some seconds, and then he replied distinctly, in a low voice,—

"I was going to tell you of my engagement to Signorlna Demarini."

There was another long silence, broken only by the sideward movement of his mother's foot on the gravel. "Well?" she said, finally.

"I know all. I saw it all, my mother!" he answered, brokenly, and then, with a repressed cry,—

"My mother! You did not! you could not! Say it to me! Say it!"

She felt herself crushed in his arms. He was holding her fiercely as though he meant to tear a denial from her.

"What—what is it that you wish me to say? You hurt me," she managed to articulate. He released her as suddenly as he had seized her, and lapsed into his former tone of dull constraint.

"I saw you with Demarini," he said, evenly.

She was silent.

"I saw him kiss you."

Still silence.

He continued, "I saw you return the kiss."

" Well ?" said his mother. He could almost have fancied that he saw her smile.

"I have challenged him," he replied.

" Well ?" she repeated. " I happen to know that you are the better swordsman."

"I do not understand," he said, with an effort,— "I do not understand how it is that you feel."

"Give the *muscadin* a lesson," suggested his mother, smiling distinctly this time.

Nadrovine stared at her. "What is it that you mean ?" he said.

She approached him. He could not keep her from touching him.

" Vladimir," she said, " is it possible,"—she paused to laugh a little under her breath,—" is it possible that you think I was serious just now ?"

" That you were serious ?" He stared at her.

" My dear Vladimir,"—she laughed uncontrolledly this time,—" my dear, dear boy, wait a moment until I tell you." He waited, without moving, until she resumed. " Nothing will give me greater pleasure, I assure you of it on my honor,"—Nadrovine winced,—" than to have you split the forearm of that caniche-haired *gommeux* in your neatest manner."

His whole body was beginning to throb with a violent although repressed disgust. There seemed to be some vile metamorphosis of heaven and earth taking place. This woman who could use the light

l　　　14*

slang of society to him at such a moment was his
mother, and her lips had just been pressed by those
of the man whom she designated "*muscadin*" and
"*gommeux.*"

"What is it? what has come to you?" he stammered. "You are different."

She stood for at least three minutes looking out
at the breaking silver of the Mediterranean, and
then, wrapping her arms in the light scarf about
her shoulders, began to speak.

"I will tell you everything," she said. "You
will be very angry. It may estrange you from me
for years, but at the end of those years you will love
me more than ever. You will feel grateful to me
as you have never felt before. It is this. I see
you on the verge of ruining your whole life, your
whole career. I determine to save you at any hazard.
You will not listen to me. I watch and find that
you are determined; that nothing can change you,—
no one,—your mother least of all. I go to see this
girl with whom you are infatuated. I find her
lovely, commonplace, the sort of woman who after
a year of marriage would drive a man to suicide.
I think, I pray, I plot. An idea comes to me. It
is a sacrifice. Ugh! I feel it now!" She made a
movement of revolt with her whole supple figure.
"It is a terrible self-sacrifice, but mothers will do
anything for their sons. I determine upon it. I
determine to do it. I nerve myself, conquer myself.

Vladimir,"—she broke off and turned to him, her face honestly anxious and eager now in the pale light,—"I saw you just now in the door-way. It was for that I let Demarini kiss me. I meant you to challenge him."

There was again silence between them.

"I do not understand," he said, finally. He noticed that the wind shaking her heavy skirts loosened from them a perfume of white lilac, which produced an unnatural effect of spring in the sultry summer air. "You say you meant me to challenge him?—that you meant me to do it?"

"Yes,—for your own good. Yes, yes. I felt that you were ruining your life,—taking your destiny into your own hands. She would have made you wretched, cramped you, thwarted you; your art would have been absolutely destroyed. There is no misery like that of an artist on finding that he has married one who does not appreciate or love his art. It is like being compelled to have for a companion in heaven one who is always sighing for earth. I saw all this. I knew I could not make you understand. I knew that you would laugh, would scorn the idea, would make a jest of it. You will perhaps hate me now for a while,—for a while: you would have hated me always if I had known this and had not told you, had not warned you, had not prevented you. You will thank me some day. How you will thank me! You will kiss my hands.

Vladimir, where are you going? Tell me that you understand. Say that you understand——"

"Do not touch me," said Nadrovine; but she followed him and took his arm into both hands.

"But you understand? you do understand?" she urged.

"Yes, I understand," he replied, in a low voice, loosing her strong fingers and putting her hands from him. "I ask that you will not disturb me now."

"Vladimir?'

"That you will not touch me."

"Vladimir, you will not always be——"

"You must not touch me. I wish to be alone. Don't follow me. I wish to be by myself."

He passed rapidly from her sight among the thickening shadows, leaving her standing there, her arms dropped straight and tense along her sides, her lips pressed inward in a firm expression of restrained pain.

Nadrovine walked rapidly until he found himself among the ruins of the little temple on the hill. The sky above was like the outreaching of a great silver wing, soft with clouds as with wind-ruffled feathers. He could see the lights in the house below, glowing like oranges of flame among the thick branches of the trees. The sea's voice seemed the purring of a somnolent tiger gentle with love and drowsing on distant sands. There was a pale,

spiritual light filtered through the floating clouds
overhead and resting on a mist of pearl below,—the
light that might shine through moonlit water upon
a drowned world. He sat perfectly still on the old
marble bench, and seemed wrapped in a banner of
sunlight, with the subtle scent of azaleas soaking
the dense air. He remembered the very folds in
her white gown. He remembered the white butterfly that had alighted on her breast. And then it
was Lotta's tea-party that he recalled,—the 'droll
little cups of red-and-gilt china, the apricot which
he had cut in three pieces, the wicked Zi-Zi who
had stolen Nicoletta's sash, Nicoletta herself, and
Lucia, and the strange anatomy of their elbowless
pink-kid arms.

" Do not be frightened, monsieur: it is only I. I
have been watching you. I thought you were asleep
until you breathed so loudly. I wished very much
to scream at first, because I did not know you; but
it was only a moment. As soon as I made up my
mind to come nearer, I recognized you immediately.
My mamma taught me that once when I was frightened by my own clothes on a chair. She took me
up to them and let me feel them; and ever since
then I have always gone up to things in the dark
and felt them or looked at them very closely. It is
such a good plan."

It was little Lotta Boutry who addressed him.
She stood with her small feet bare on the cool marble

in front of him. Her night-gown made a lawny
vapor about her fragile limbs, and the moonlight
glanced from her veil of dark hair in lustrous daz-
zles, as from the leaves of the great magnolia below
them. She looked like the spirit of this pale, opal-
tinted night condensed into human shape.

XV.

"I hope I did not startle you, monsieur?" she
continued, pushing back her damp hair and regarding him earnestly without moving.

"Startle me? Why, no," replied Nadrovine,
absently. "But your slippers, little one? You
will take cold standing on that chilly marble."

"Oh, I think not," said Lotta. "It feels delicious,—not at all too cool. The night is so warm
in the house. I was thinking that the moon looked
hot as I came up the stairway. I saw it through a
little tear in the clouds. It was like a hot coal
through gray ashes."

"But what are you doing here at this hour of the
night, little one?" asked Nadrovine.

"I came for my poor Zi-Zi. I forgot him. He
has been lying there alone ever since five o'clock
this afternoon. He was so unhappy that I could
not make up my mind to strangle him, even though
Cousine Ilva gave me one of her gold hairs. I
know he has been thinking, thinking, thinking out
here all by himself. Because dolls must think, you

know. I am sure that locomotives do. I am sure
they are in a wicked mood when they run off the
rails and hurt so many poor people; and then when
they run together—what they call a collision—I am
sure that they are in love with each other and that
they are determined to embrace each other no matter
how many people they hurt. I am sure dolls have
feelings. If one could alive them with steam, like
locomotives, I am sure they would run into each
other's arms, no matter how terribly they pinched
the fingers of the person who was holding them.
I will get poor Zi-Zi and try to comfort him."

She returned with the little doll in his crimson
velvet blouse pressed against her bosom.

"He is very, very sad," she said, gravely. "His
whole face is wet, he has been weeping so. You
know more about men than I do, monsieur: tell
me how to comfort him."

"There is no comfort for men's tears, little one."

"But Zi-Zi is only a doll-man. There must be
some comfort for him. Suppose *you* hold him a
little while. I must go back to bed before they
put out the lights. There is no light in Cousine
Ilva's room, and I crept out on my toes to keep
from waking her. I could see her in the moonlight,
though. She is so lovely. She let me put all the
dolls to sleep across our feet, and did not even move,
and she let me cover them with her pretty white-
and-blue toilet-cover. I slipped out of bed very

softly. She did not even stir. Her hair was all between us, like gold. I kissed it. I wanted to kiss her, but I was afraid I would wake her. She said something in her sleep. She looked like an angel. Her hair showed on each side like gold wings. Oh, monsieur, you would write a story about her if you could see her to-night."

Nadrovine drew the child into his arms, but he was trembling, and she shrank back alarmed.

"What is it? why do you shake so? Do you see anything? Never mind, though: I can control myself. Perhaps it is a fairy."

"And so you left her asleep, little one?"

"There is nothing, then? I thought you saw something. Yes, she was fast, fast asleep. She taught me such a pretty verse before she went to sleep, though. I only remember two lines. It was all about different eyes. These are the lines:

> Quick to change are eyes of blue,
> Brown's of all the sweetest hue.

And then she said, 'Do you know any one with brown eyes, *chérie?*' and I said that you had brown eyes, and she laughed and held me. I was pulling off her stockings. It is so pretty to do,—just like peeling the dark-blue skin off of a white fig; and she has such pretty little toes,—the nails shine like any one else's finger-nails, and there are little white arches on them. Then I comb and brush her hair.

She is like a big, big doll to me. I do love her so!
You love her, don't you, monsieur?"

"Yes," said Nadrovine.

"I was sure that you did. And she loves you,—
oh, devotedly!"

"*Chérie*, how do you know?"

"Because when I speak of you she comes nearer
to me, and takes me in her arms, and keeps her face
against mine so that I cannot see it. And whenever
your name is mentioned she turns as if it were her
own name and some one were calling her. And—
and the princes in her fairy-stories always look like
you, and when she draws pictures they are all like
you. And it was she who made me think of praying
for you with those whom I love. And one day when
I said to her that I hoped she would marry you,
she almost hurt me with kisses, but whispered afterwards, 'Do not say that to any one else, darling, for
they would not understand.' But it is true. I do
hope that you will be married, and then I would
pay you long, long visits, and we would be so
happy together. You would wish it, would you
not?"

"With all my heart, pretty one. But see, the
lights are going out in the house. You must not
stay longer. Will you take your cousin a little message from me? And can I trust you to tell it to no
one else?"

The child looked at him seriously while stroking

H   15

the disconsolate Zi-Zi down the entire length of his inaccurately-formed little figure.

" Must I awaken her to tell her, monsieur ?"

" Yes,—with a kiss, little one. Tell her where you have been, and that you have seen me, and then say to her the words that I will repeat to you."

" But, monsieur, she has such lovely, lovely dreams; and the next morning she always tells them to me. Suppose I should break one in the middle? One can never mend a dream, you know, no matter how much one may desire to. One may begin by dreaming of a nest of little white doves with pink bills and feet, which one is feeding on stars that taste sweet like bon-bons, and one may be awakened and go to sleep again to dream of a large cat that has eyes of green fire and red-hot claws which scratch and burn at the same time. I really know, monsieur, because I have had such things happen, and it is so distressing. And then, too, Cousine Ilva's dreams are so beautiful. She hears water falling like music that makes itself. And sees flowers whose perfumes are so sweet that to them it is like loving. And great, silver-white peacocks, with purple-and-gold eyes on their tails. And jewels poured out on the ground, which are the lovely thoughts of good little children that the angels turn into precious stones to feed the poor. The sapphires are one's thoughts of the blessed Christ-Child, and the pearls of the Holy Spirit, and the rubies of God. And when one wishes to help others it is diamonds, and when one is sorry for one's sins it is emeralds. And amethysts mean kisses to those who do not expect them. And a topaz is just a kind word, even if one only speaks it to one's self and nobody hears. And there are many, many others; but I forget. Oh, I could not bear to disturb one of her dreams, monsieur!"

"No, my sweet one, I can well believe it; although such souls have beautiful dreams whether they wake or sleep. But you will tell her the words I say to you as soon as she wakes, will you not?"

"Yes, yes, truly," said the child, earnestly. "What are they? I must hurry, and I wish to learn them correctly."

"Say to her, then, my little heart, that the words on the blue ring that she wears around her neck are part of my message to her, and ask her to trust me whatever happens; that, whatever it is, it could not be avoided. And"—he held the child's face in his hands, so that he could look into her eyes—"and that I love her, that I will always love her."

"I am sure that you do," said the child, simply. "It makes your face so good."

Nadrovine carried her in his arms down the stairs and to the edge of the last terrace. As he put her gently down she kissed him of her own accord, a little, damp, child's kiss that went to his heart. He kneeled down and drew her against his breast for a last caress.

"Good-by, my dear little Lotta," he said. "And say your little prayer for me twice to-night."

"I will, monsieur. But I have already said it once."

"Then make it three times, my dear little true one, and it will help me when I am sad and troubled."

"Dear monsieur," she replied, agitated vaguely, her lips quivering, "my prayers will be that sadness and trouble may not come to you."

"One might as well pray against the coming of death, little one. But there, I am talking at random. Run, run, before the last light is put out. I will wait here for you."

He gave her a last kiss, and then stood watching her airy figure until it was gathered into the evasive shadows of the old garden. It seemed to him as though she were the wraith of his youth, vanishing as he looked, and leaving behind only a pulsing gloom and the yearning sounds of a summer midnight. The great harmony of the sea wounded him, as we are wounded by a voice that sang at the funeral of one we loved. It was the sound most associated with her,—with her words, her tears, her laughter,—a profound, subdued undercurrent of rich cadences, above which her clear tones rose like the night-call of a bird above the sonorous breathing of a great forest. He stood and looked at the pauseless swaying of the moonlit tide below him, and knew that he could never again endure that majestic sight nor bear the rhythm of its throbbing monotone. It is hard to be deprived of love and of the sea at the same time,— only those who love the sea can understand how hard. Nadrovine's heart surged up for one bitter instant in a passion of revolt and rebellion, that instinct of savagery which possesses us when we first learn that circumstance is lord of all, and that the result of the actions of others, and not man, is often master of his fate. He had not allowed himself to think of his mother, or, rather, as yet he felt nothing in regard to her. That part of his nature which used to vibrate at the least memory of her seemed numbed and incapable of sensation. He walked back and forth along the broad turf-path, with that hungry feeling growing in his heart which besets those who walk alone through scenes where their dearest have once been with them. And then he became racked with an unconquerable longing to see her, to speak with her, to take her in his arms, if only for one moment. To know that it was impossible only rendered the painful longing more frantic. He thought, with a sharp contraction of regret, of how many better messages he might have given the child to take her, and in so much sweeter a way. At least he could have sent her a knot of her favorite blush-roses: they would have lain on her pillow all night and in the morning have been pressed against her face. But this thought disturbed him with a sudden sense of revulsion. Ah! he remembered. He paused, and

15*

stood perfectly still, lifting his shoulders a little, as though to withstand the buffet of an inrolling wave. His mind wandered to commonplace things. He remembered that his man had neglected to replace some books, which were to be returned, in the packing-cases. The petty prick of irritation returned with the thought. They should have been sent back at least two days ago. There was also a roll of proof waiting for him on his writing-table. He began reconsidering a chapter which he had determined to omit. The sea came rolling towards him, insistent, unavoidable, like a great genie daring him to forget for even a moment. Turning, he walked steadily in the opposite direction, but those dithyrambic surges of deep sound, beating up against the steely arch overhead, seemed to descend upon him in great floods, and to inundate his mind with their individuality, until he was powerless to think any thoughts save those which they recalled.

XVI.

It was at seven o'clock the next morning that Madame Nadrovine was roused by the entrance of some one who walked softly through the gloom of the closely-curtained room until reaching her bed-side.

"Alma?" she said, half raising herself among the light bedclothes, "is it not very early for my coffee?" There was no reply, but the intruder suddenly thrust wide the venetian blinds of the window facing the bed, and drew back the curtains, admitting a tangle of early sunbeams, which, reflected from a bath near the window, played over the bed and the half-awakened woman. She put up one arm to shield her eyes, leaning on the other. Her hair was braided in one great braid, like that of a little girl. She looked amazingly young, with her bare throat, blinking eyes, and cheeks flushed with sleep and creased by the folds of her pillow-case like those of a baby.

"What is it? Who is it? What do you want?" she asked, unable yet to identify the person who confronted her.

"He is dead! I have killed him," replied the voice of Nadrovine. He was standing with his back to the window, and she could not see his face for the blaze of morning light behind him.

"I have killed him," he repeated, in the same monotonous voice. "I only meant to wound him; but he slipped. He was quite dead in a few moments. The surgeon could do nothing."

His mother stammered, catching her night-gown together at the throat:

"Who is dead? who is dead? What do you mean?"

"It is Demarini. We fought before day this morning. The sun was just rising when he died. There was a horrible likeness with the eyes shut. She is so fair, but there is a likeness. It was horrible. I can never forget it. I will see that face over your shoulder whenever I look at you."

"Bah!—I will not believe it, that he is dead," cried his mother, making an excited motion to leave the bed. "It is some ridiculous sensationalism. One knows the way that surgeons talk,—and an Italian! Ring for Alma."

"No," replied Nadrovine. "I have locked the door. I wish to speak to you alone. It seems so strange. I seem so changed, as though I myself were dead. You know that you have ruined my life?"

"My dear boy, let me——"

"When I say that you have ruined my life, I mean that you have also ruined everything that makes life worth living. You have left me nothing."

"My dear Vladimir——"

"I no longer love you. I would prefer the pain of loving you, knowing you to be unworthy, rather than this feeling of utter incapacity. You seem like a machine,—a beautiful machine which has maimed a man confiding too much in his knowledge of it. Nothing seems real but this hour, this moment. My boyhood and manhood are like the confusion of past dreams. I know that you are my mother, that you gave me birth with pain and have sacrificed much for me, and yet I hope that after to-day I will never look at you or hear your voice again. I know that this absolute absence of all emotion is unnatural. Nature will speak before long, perhaps before to-night, with another of her million voices. Perhaps I shall hate you. I might be tempted to curse you." There was a pause, during which one could hear a gardener's boy sweeping the grass with a broom of twigs. His mother made no reply, but continued to look up at him with her clear, unfaltering eyes.

"Well?" she said, at last.

"I am going before such a change can take place. I wished to see you once more. It will be a final farewell. I hope never to see you again."

"You will say that, of course, as often as you wish," she murmured behind her shut teeth. "Go on."

"I thought that perhaps it might soften me, that I might find something to say to you,—something forgiving. I do not forgive you."

"And then?"

"I will never forgive you. We will never see each other again."

"You will remember that I told you we might be estranged for several years."

"You will never see me again. You will never even hear of me."

"It is natural that you should feel bitter. I expected you to be much more violent. But it is nonsense—about Demarini, you know. Naturally, he swooned from loss of blood."

"There is no doubt of his being dead," said Na-

m

drovine, coldly. "I came to speak to you of one or two things. In the first place, I wish to ask that you will make no effort to discover my whereabouts at any time. It would only annoy and disturb me, and would change nothing."

"He speaks to me,—to me!" whispered his mother, still keeping her eyes fastened on him. She nodded assent.

"Then I wish you to allow Ivan to pack everything that I leave, without being interrupted. I want no one to enter my rooms or arrange my things except Ivan."

Again his mother nodded.

"And then there is this. You have a portrait of my father. It is in a carved silver case set with little rubies. Ah! it is there around your neck. Give it to me, please."

She bared her throat with a superb movement.

"Take it," she replied.

He unfastened it without touching her white flesh, and opened it to assure himself that all was as he remembered it. His own face confronted him,—the face of a boy of eighteen, with blond curls, rather long. A sudden rush of emotion mastered him. He was blinded, and the blood gathered hotly in his throat. He put out his hand to steady himself, and it fell upon his mother's shoulder. She clasped it with both her own, in a sudden eager gesture of appeal. Her lips moved.

Nadrovine stood staring down at the portrait in his hand, while she watched him ravenously, her parted lips still forming unuttered words.

"He is softened. It has touched him. My great love has melted him. He will forgive me."

These were the sentences that she framed in silent but rapturous certainty. He turned suddenly, withdrawing his hand from beneath hers, and tossing the open case upon the bed.

"It has always been so. You have always put me before him. I never knew it until now. I might have known. I might have known that such lightheartedness as yours could never have been feigned. What woman who loved her husband could have laughed and danced and reigned, as you have done, with him, her husband, rotting in Siberia? I have been a fool! I have been a fool!"

He went to the door and unlocked it. She thought that he would come back, but he opened it and passed through, closing it after him.

"It is a natural mood. It will pass," she said, consoling herself by speaking aloud as she rose from bed.

She walked to the open window and half closed the blinds, shutting out the sunlight. There was a half-finished letter on her writing-table, — an order for some new morning gowns. She took up the pen and began to finish it mechanically, thinking of other things all the while that she wrote. Not for an

instant did she believe Demarini to be dead. All
the frivolous details that she was describing inter-
wove themselves oddly with her thoughts, and the
scenes of the past twenty-four hours appeared again
to her, seen through folds of lace and muslin and
behind the fluttering of pale-green ribbons, and hats
garnished with apple-blossoms. She ended the letter
and sealed it with elaborate care, spoiling two or three
envelopes in the process, and then reopened it to say
that, after all, she had decided to have the gown of
India muslin made over pale-green silk and embroidered by hand with apple-blossoms in a very delicate
shade of rose-color, the sprays being far apart in
order to give the costume an airy look. She then
sealed it again, even more carefully than before, and
rang for her maid, being impatient to dress and yet
avoiding beginning. It seemed as though she could
not take her bath and have her hair arranged for
hours; and all the time she was wondering about
Nadrovine, and picturing him in various ways.

It was not until she appeared at luncheon and
asked for him that she realized his determination.
He had taken the morning train for Paris some
hours ago. The servant who told her noticed that
she assumed her seat at the table rather abruptly,
but beyond this she showed no emotion. The only
time that her self-control forsook her was when she
became convinced beyond doubt of Demarini's death.
Instead of growing pale, the blood rushed darkly to

her face, which worked convulsively in an expression of horror. They heard her mutter,—

"Then he will not forgive me."

Her maid wished to undress her, but she motioned her fiercely to leave the room. The girl, who adored her, crouching outside her door, heard the soft footfalls moving up and down for at least two hours, and the noise of her silken skirt hissing in little jerks as her quick impatient strides drew it after her along the tiled floor.

XVII.

Three weeks of unbroken silence from Nadrovine followed the day of his departure. His mother had not left the house once, and for forty-eight hours had been locked in her apartments. No one was admitted. The trays of food left at her door were taken away untouched, while the little Swede, kneeling and listening at the key-hole, could hear nothing,—not a movement, not a sound, not even a sigh.

It was about nine o'clock on the evening of the third day, that Alma, passing through the hall with wine and fruit in her hands, encountered a figure clothed in white standing just within the door of entrance. She stopped and stared in silence, while the figure approached her. It spoke in a soft voice.

"Can I see Madame Nadrovine?"

Alma saw that there was pale-golden hair under its scarf of white gauze, and that its breast rose and fell quickly. She also heard the sound of its escaping breath, and decided that this breathing was too rapid and natural to be that of an apparition.

"Can I see your mistress?" said the gentle voice a second time.

Alma steadied her tray of wine and fruit against the carved iron railing of the stairway.

"I do not think so, mademoiselle," she replied, hesitating. "She has not seen any one, not even taken food, for three days."

"Is she then ill?"

"No one knows, mademoiselle; for no one has seen her for three days."

"I must see her," said Ilva.

"But, mademoiselle——"

"I must see her," repeated the girl, gently. "Come! you will take me to her, I know. I am in great sorrow, and she alone can help me."

Alma still hesitated, although she began to yield, and Ilva took her little, plump, tanned hand in both her own and pressed it against her breast. "I may be able to help her too," she said. "Give me the wine and fruit, and let me take it to her."

"But—but——" stammered the girl. Ilva, coming close to her and still holding her hands, said, in a ringing voice, low and sweet with the weakness of misery,—

"Listen! listen, my sister,—for all women should be sisters in time of trouble: I only want to help her and to try to be helped by her. I am in great

sorrow. My wretchedness is almost past my own
power of comprehension. I wish only to stand outside her door and speak to her. You may watch
here on the stairs. Why, what harm could I do
her? I am only a poor, unhappy girl. Her door
is locked, you say. How could I harm her in any
way? How could I? Even if I wanted to, how
could I? And what is your name?"

"Alma," replied the girl.

"Then, dear, dear Alma, let me go to her door
and speak to her through it. You may watch; you
may even listen, if you wish."

The girl broke suddenly into tears.

"Go! go!" she exclaimed, sobbing, and holding
out the little silver tray with both hands, while avert-
ing her face. "Go quickly, and the blessed Lord be
with you!"

"And with you!" said Ilva, kissing her. She
took the wine and fruit from her hands, saying, with
a sorrowful smile, "But why do you weep?"

"I weep because you have the look in your face
of those who die young," replied the girl, "and
because you are so beautiful."

"It is well to die young," said Ilva, smiling again.
"But I love you for your tears, and I will pray for
you always with those whom I love."

She kissed her again solemnly on the forehead,
and ascended the wide marble stairway. Alma had
told her to stop at the first door to the right, and she

stood there awhile in silence, before speaking. Then she said, gently,—

"Vladimir's mother?"

There was only silence for reply.

She spoke again, even more softly, more gently:

"Vladimir's mother? Vladimir's dear, dear mother?"

Only silence, profound, vibrating. Again she spoke, with an anguished note of entreaty beginning to throb through her low tones:

"Oh, will you not answer me? Will you not answer me? I only wish to ask you where he is, that I may tell him how fully I forgive him,—how I believed the words that little Lotta brought me. I trust him. I trust him utterly. I feel that he is suffering, that he is in anguish! I only can help him,—but not without you,—not without you. Even if you hate me, will you not open to me for his sake? You may curse me, you may tell me how you hate me, but I will not care. It is for his sake. . . . Oh, if you would but understand! Oh, if I could but make you understand! I will go into a convent. I will promise you néver to see him again. Only I cannot bear the thought of his suffering: I cannot! . . . I cannot! It is driving me mad. I hear only evil words of him from morning until night, from night until morning. Will you not answer me? Are you dead too?"

Still the heavy silence which seemed to press

against her ears until they ached. She kneeled down, supporting the tray of fruit upon her knees and lifting upward her pale face in supplication.

"O Sancta Maria," she whispered, "soften her heart; let her heart be softened by the words that thou wilt teach me to say to her."

Again she bent forward, with her cheek against the door.

"Open to me in *his* name,—in *his* name," she murmured. "I only wish it for his sake. Believe me! oh, believe me,—believe me! You may say what you will to me. I will endure any reproach that you offer me. Only open to me. Only open to me, that I may see you and speak with you."

After waiting several moments, during which her lips moved incessantly in whispered words of prayer, she spoke again:

"I will not weary you more; but if during the night you feel that you can speak to me, open the door. You will find me still here. And there is wine for you,—his dear mother,—and some fruit. Oh, you must be so weak,—so weak! My heart aches when I think of it. But now good-night. May angels minister to you! May you be told in dreams of my sincerity! I am ready to promise whatever you wish."

She then stretched herself deliberately along the floor, resting her head against a panther's skin, which she rolled up and over which she placed her gauze

scarf in order to have a comparatively cool pillow.
It seemed to her that she lay there for hours. She
lived over again every scene with Nadrovine since
her first meeting with him as a little girl. Alma
had fallen asleep on the stairs, and the wax candles
in the hall below, unextinguished, dripped in semi-
transparent mounds on the tiles beneath and hung
in stalactites from the crystal bobèches. One by one
they burned low, flared, and went out. Only the
languid glittering of the stars which studded the
space of sky enclosed by an open window near at
hand lighted the great hall. Ilva had not stirred.
She·lay in an attitude of tense quiet, one hand retaining her improvised pillow in its place, the other
stretched above the little tray at her side, like the
hand of a mother questioning the slumber of her
first-born. Was it not this wine and fruit which
was to nourish his mother,—the woman who had
·brought him into the world to love her and to be
loved by her?

It was one o'clock when the door opened wide, and
a tall, impassive form appeared on the threshold,
pressed forward, as it were, by a flood of light from
beyond. The folds of her white crape dressing-
gown fell in an almost forbidding simplicity to her
bare feet. Her face was ghastly, her eyes dull and
sunken beneath their dark lids. Her thick hair,
half braided, was tangled in a lustreless mesh of
strands.

Ilva at once rose to her knees, and remained in that position, looking up at her. Presently she ventured to lift her clasped hands timidly, drawing them down at once and straining them against her breast.

"Oh, how ill you look! How ill you look!" she exclaimed, in a pained voice.

Nadrovine's mother stood motionless, still regarding her. Suddenly she moved aside.

"Come in!" she said, sternly.

Ilva found herself in an airy room, charming with hangings of white and gold, and with low chairs and couches covered with old-fashioned silks in faded tints. The bed, with its eight curtains of yellow brocade, was as smooth as though just spread. There were torn papers scattered over the floor, and an overturned inkstand. The ink, sluggishly following an uncertain course, had left a gloomy stain on the bright floor.

"And now, what is it that you wish with me?" asked the woman.

Ilva's heart seemed strangling her.

"That you will tell me where he is. I wish to forgive him. I wish to know where he is. It is only because I cannot bear that he shall suffer. Ah! I know that you will tell me," she ended, in a suffocating voice.

Madame Nadrovine regarded her calmly. "I know no more where he is than you do," she said, at last.

"But, signora!—dear signora . . . !"

"I have told you that I know no more than you do."

"But you love him?—you love him? You cannot desire that he should suffer. If he could only know that I forgive him!"

"For what do you forgive him?"

"Signora, . . . for the death of my father."

"You are indeed lenient, mademoiselle."

"I trust him. I know that it was not his fault. I do not understand, but I am sure of that. I trust him utterly. I am sure that he did not mean to do it."

"'I have not found so great faith, no, not in Israel!'" quoted the woman, in a hard voice, half smiling down at her. "You are deeply in love, it is evident, mademoiselle."

"Oh, yes! yes!" cried Ilva, her face breaking into a radiance of innocent rapture. "You must see how I love him to have come to you. I felt that you hated me, and yet I came. I loved him so much that your hate seemed a little, little thing in comparison. I knew that you would see me. I was sure of it. I thought perhaps that I could make you understand that you had hated me unjustly,—that I was not as you thought me. Believe me, signora, oh, believe me! I love you for *his* sake, in spite of your hatred. I will do whatever you wish."

"I tell you that I know nothing. Why do you stare at me so? There, sit down. You are as white as your gown. There, sit down, I say. Do you faint? Look! I will shake you if you attempt to faint."

She caught the girl fiercely by the arm, while the great eyes looked up at her, dazed, but unterrified.

"You would not really hurt me?" she said, half questioningly. Madame Nadrovine withdrew her hand in some haste.

"Why should I hurt you?" she asked.

"I knew you would not. It was only a thought. We cannot help our thoughts, you know." Then suddenly she slipped from the chair into which Madame Nadrovine had forced her, and clasped her about with both arms.

"Signora! signora! in Christ's name,—for Christ's sake,—tell me where he is!"

"Little idiot! have I not already said twice, that I do not know?"

"But, signora . . . "

"I tell you I do not know."

"But, signora, think,—think!"

"I say I know nothing,—nothing! Saints! am I not sufficiently humiliated by such a confession, that you force me to repeat it? I tell you that I know nothing. Do you hear? Nothing, nothing, nothing, nothing!"

"But, signora, listen. I wish to . . . "

"Nothing, I say! Let me go! You drive me frantic! Let go!"

She drew her robe violently from the girl's hands, causing her to swerve and fall sidelong on the floor. A little sigh escaped the pale lips, and then the slight limbs settled quietly.

The woman stood looking at her for a moment, rigid, fierce, her hands clinched; but she soon saw by the pallor of the face at her feet that the swoon was not a feigned one. She knelt abruptly, and took one of the little, relaxed hands in hers. It was damp and cold. She put her hand on the wavy hair: it was also damp about the brow and temples.

"Wake! wake!" she called, in a stertorous whisper, dragging her upward by the lifeless arms, and then lowering the inert body again upon the floor. She slapped her face, her hands. She poured the contents of a great ebony case of perfume over the inanimate breast. The delicate hue of flesh shone through the soaked muslin, but no signs of returning life stirred its folds. She then caught sight of the decanter of wine on the tray near the still open door, and, seizing it, forced a glassful between the girl's teeth. As the long breath of returning consciousness lifted her bosom, the fasting woman at her side, made ravenous by the smell of the wine and fruit, began to eat the grapes, skins and seed, tearing them from their stems with her sharp teeth, and washing them down with glass after glass of sherry.

XVIII.

When she had finished this strange and hurried repast, she turned, still kneeling, and looked down at the prostrate girl. Ilva's eyes were closed, but she breathed regularly, and one of her hands stirred slightly, like a fallen magnolia-leaf lifted by the wind. Madame Nadrovine felt the girl's heart. It was beating, slowly but firmly.

"Let me help you to the bed," she suggested, in a cold voice. Ilva did not reply. She closed again her dark eyes, which she had half opened, and lay without motion. Madame Nadrovine did not waste further time in words. Thrusting her strong arms under the slight figure, she lifted her and carried her to the great bed, with its eight shining curtains.

She drew the old-fashioned embroidered white satin coverlet from beneath her, and placed it over her up to her breast.

"I thank you," murmured Ilva, again opening her languid eyes for an instant. Invigorated by the wine which she had drunk, Madame Nadrovine began to rub the lifeless limbs with a regular sweeping movement of her strong hands, and as she sat, bending back and forth to her task, she noticed how frail and wasted was the fair face and how transparent the little hands unfolded on the shimmering coverlet.

"She has been fasting too," she muttered to herself in her voice of the past three weeks,—a voice

without feeling or inflections. She found that she
could not withdraw her gaze from the quiet, pale
face. What long, dark lashes she had, curling to
her eyebrows with their golden tips which a *mon-
daine* would undoubtedly have dyed! What fine,
narrow eyebrows! What a clear forehead, smooth
and bluish, with thread-like veins at the temples!
Her soft hair grew in little points, downy and of a
pale brown. Above rippled a luxurious tide of
silverish gold. The little nostrils were haughty,
thin, and high-arched, the lips curved and drooping
slightly at the corners. Nadrovine's mother gazed
at them as though under a spell, and then her look
dropped to the white throat stretched back on the
pillow. Her little crooked toilet-scissors were lying
near. She could touch them with her outstretched
hand. What was it that she had said to Nadrovine
only a month ago? She took them up on three
fingers and made the motion of cutting in the air.
The sherry burned through her veins. A soft touch
roused her. Ilva had slipped from the pillow, and
was resting her cheek upon one of her hands.

"You are so good to me," she said. "I knew
that you were good. He could not love you as he
does if you were not good."

Madame Nadrovine let the scissors drop noiselessly
among the folds of her dressing-gown. She frowned,
however.

"You are clever," she remarked, in her harshest

tones. "I made a mistake when I thought you silly."

"No, no, signora! Do not think I say things for effect. He used to speak to me for hours and hours of his love for you. We used to talk of you over and over again. I was afraid, but he used to tell me of your loveliness and goodness, and then I would not be so frightened. Ah, signora, why do you hate me? He will always be yours more than mine. He is your flesh and blood. You have suffered for him. Oh, signora, think of it!—you have suffered for him, and I, no matter how much I suffer, what can I do for him? We are separated forever. He will not marry me with this stain of blood between us. Will you not let me love you? I can have no more. He will never wish me to be his wife now: all that is gone,—gone. I can only be his sister, —your daughter, signora,—your daughter!"

For the first time she began to weep. Great tears glazed her face. Her sobs shook her convulsively, and she grasped Madame Nadrovine's gown with both hands. The woman rose excitedly, pushing her back among the heaped-up pillows.

"Never!... never!" she said, in a choked voice. "My daughter? Never!"

She took two or three strides forward. In the centre of the room she paused, turning about and regarding the tear-shaken girl with a splendid scorn.

"My daughter! Are you Demarini's child, you

who wish to be my daughter? You wish to have
for a mother the mother of the man who killed your
father?"

"Ah, signora, that was an accident. My poor
father slipped. We were told that by the surgeon
who attended him. And I also have *his* words,—
the words of your son. They are here in my breast.
It was an accident, a terrible, terrible accident. Oh,
signora, believe that I have suffered. I loved my
father. It was I who watched with him all that first
dreadful night,—I and little Lotta. She would not
leave me. There was no one else but the servants;
and of course I could not have borne that. My
mother and my aunt were both ill, and Nini is afraid
of the dead. I sat beside him, at his head, so that I
could look down upon his face. It was very beautiful. I never noticed before how long his lashes were,
like a woman's, and his forehead so clear in the
candle-light. At first I could only think of the
awful wound in his breast, . . . of who had made
it there. I felt as though the sword had pierced me.
And then to be thrust by the hand that had caressed
me,—his daughter!—that had drawn the sign of
the cross upon my lips, and in my tears! I knew
that my father had forgiven him. He looked so
calm, . . . so good. It was almost the face of a saint,
—so pure and placid. And he *was* good,—good and
gentle. It must have been some madness. I know
that he has forgiven. I know that he would plead

·for me, signora, . . . would wish me to forgive.
Why, I can almost see him, there, there beyond your
shoulder——"

In her excitement, with running tears and catching breath, Ilva kneeled up in the great bed and
extended her arm towards Madame Nadrovine, her
eyes fixed as though on some object beyond her.
The short, hoarse cry that the woman uttered
startled her: it was almost like the bark of some
animal in anguish. She wheeled and caught at a
chair near her for support.

"You see nothing! . . . Why do you point at me
in that theatrical manner? . . . You know that you
see nothing! . . . You do it for effect." The words
came in hurried bursts, as though forced from her,
and the chair trembled with her heavy grasp upon it.

"It is absurd, . . . absurd!" she repeated, sinking
down and thrusting back her loosened hair with both
hands. "But you are a good actress, mademoiselle."

At these words, Ilva rose slowly from the bed,
and stood erect, meeting the sneering gaze of
Madame Nadrovine in a calm, level look.

"Since you can believe this of me, there is nothing
left for me but to go, signora," she said, with a quiet
dignity. "I wish you good-night."

She made a slight inclination, graceful and self-
contained, and, passing through the open door, went
swiftly down the broad stairway and into the warm
night outside. Madame Nadrovine remained where

she was, the scornful smile with which she had greeted the last speech of the young girl still lifting the corners of her lips.

As she had done with Nadrovine, she waited, expecting to see Ilva return and throw herself at her feet in a last paroxysm of pleading and despair. The moments passed on in quiet silence, however, the perfumes and leaf-sounds of the great garden below rising and falling with the indolent wind. She rose finally and approached the open window. In the distant haze of the late and waning moonlight, the girl's figure shone like a small statuette of silver among the dark shrubbery, and presently vanished altogether. Madame Nadrovine turned again towards the lighted room. It was suffocating with the scent of the vervain which she had poured over Ilva during her swoon, and the empty grapetwigs lay in a desolate-looking bundle among the half-filled sherry-glasses. Moths and strange summer insects of all sorts were fluttering and singing about the glittering candles on her toilet-table and writing-desk. Some of them were half burned to death and buzzed in anguish among the silver and ivory brushes and toilet-articles; others, half plunged in the melted wax, strove to free themselves with desperate contortions of their long legs.

The woman stood for a moment gazing absently down at the struggling creatures; then, lifting a brush, she put an end to their pain by a quick tap or two, and, taking fresh candles from a drawer, placed them on her writing-table. A square book of black Russian leather with a heavy lock and monogram in silver lay between the two candle-sticks. She opened it, read a page or two, turned to a fresh page, dipped her pen in the ink, and, kneeling down in front of the table, began to write as follows:

"Just God, have mercy upon me, and turn the heart of my son towards me again. Thou knowest that all I have done was for his sake. Thou knowest how distasteful and abominable it was to me beyond words. If I have done wrong I ask Thy forgive-ness. I will fast for a year, and sell my jewels for the poor, if Thou wilt but pardon me. Judge me not by the offence, O Lord, but by the love that caused it. If I almost worship my son, O Lord, Thou, whose Son was worshipped by his mother, wilt look leniently upon what for me is a sin. O God, lay not the death of Demarini to my charge. Thou knowest that I did not mean him to be killed. My object was to make a breach between the two families which would prevent my son from marrying an immature child in no way worthy of him. My God, I have been called a hard woman. Thou who madest me knowest that if this is so it is the fault of heredity rather than from any wish of my own; but to my son, O God, I am as melted wax. Lord, give him back to me, if I die with his first look.

Give him back to me in love, if his first kiss means death to me. These words are weak and cold to what is filling my heart like bubbling iron. Why didst Thou send this girl to divide us? Did I not bring him up to fear and honor Thee? Did I not teach him to make his genius an offering unto Thee? Wherein have I failed? Why is this punishment sent upon me? I feel that Thou art angry with me; and yet, Lord, it is not, alas! Thy anger which so much grieves me as the loss of my son. It is not so much Thy anger that I dread, as that it will cause Thee to keep him from me. I feel that Thou art displeased with me for my lack of gentleness to the girl; but I would have been a hypocrite had I pretended to feel any pity for her. Perhaps she deserves it. I do not know. It is nothing to me. Thou seest, O Lord, how utterly I bare my soul to Thee. I hide nothing. I excuse nothing. The thing that I did was wrong, but the love that caused it was sublime. It was the wisdom of the world, but Thy Son hath told us to be 'wise as serpents,' and I did not mean to be less 'harmless than a dove.' I meant not the death of any one. I only wished to save my son, and the great genius which Thou hast given him, from a living death. Let him live to thank me for it. Let him live to recognize that Demarini's death was indeed an accident for which neither he nor I are responsible. Bring him back to me. Soften his heart. Give him to me again.

Thou knowest that, with all my sins, I am honest to Thee. Even to Thee I never feign to feel that which is absent. I fear Thee more than I love Thee, and I love my son more than I desire perfect goodness, but if Thou wilt only give him to me once more I will strive to serve Thee even with my hardness. Give him back to me, that I may hear him say, if only once, that he loves me, and then punish me as Thou wilt. Amen."

XIX.

Madame Nadrovine, with the practicality which distinguished her, set about aiding Providence to answer her prayer. She employed in secret the services of one of the most distinguished detectives in France, and, some months from the night of her interview with Ilva, discovered that her son was ill with a slow fever in poor apartments in one of the side-streets of Paris.

She knocked at the door of his room the day after this information had reached her, scarcely waiting for his answer before entering. It was a small room, with whitewashed walls and heavy walnut furniture of that awkward and obsolete order which always manages to rise, like cream, to the top story of old houses. The windows were small, set with panes of greenish glass, and spotted a dingy yellow over the entire upper sash by repeated layers of rain-drops. Opposite, in the waterish light of the fading

afternoon, the zinc roofs and awnings gave forth a
gray glare, which seemed to be reflected in the black
ooze of the streets below. A fine and steady rain
was falling. The depressing gleam of hundreds of
soaked umbrellas passing and repassing far below
gave one a sensation of desolation which was aug-
mented by the glisten of the wet cab-tops, and the
swallows preening their damp feathers on the branch
of a dead tree near the grimy window.

Sunk in an old chair covered with time-dimmed
cretonne, was Nadrovine, his face turned listlessly
towards the blank patch of sky visible to him through
the clouded casement, his hands resting inertly on
a closed book which was sunk between his knees.
His dark dressing-gown, folded and re-folded about
his figure, gave a wonderful appearance of emacia-
tion. His hair, grown longer during his illness, recalled to his face a look of his youth as represented in
the miniature which he had taken from his mother's
neck on the day of their last interview. She turned
the key in the door, which she closed behind her,
and, slipping it into her pocket, advanced a few steps.

She spoke to him. " Vladimir?" she said, in a
low voice.

He half rose from the great chair, steadying himself with a hand on either arm. His pale face became suffused with blood.

" It is you? . . . It is you?" he said, on short,
rushing breaths.

" Yes, it is I ! . . . your mother. Did you think
that you could be ill, suffering, and I not find it
out ?"

He continued to stare at her in silence, his quivering arms retaining him in his half-erect posture.

She came close to him and put forth her hand to
force him gently back into the chair, but he dropped
from her touch and pressed back among the worn-out
springs, making them creak with his sudden energy
of sickness.

" I ask you not to touch me !" he panted.

" But you cannot expect me to obey you, dear great
one ?" she said, bending over him, with the smile
which no other had ever seen. " It is the fancy of
an invalid,—such a dear invalid ! . . . But you have
been too much alone, my darling !"

She attempted to run her long fingers through his
hair.

" I beg of you . . . " he reiterated, in the tone
of one exquisitely tortured.

" Ah, great one, great one, if you knew the anguish
you make me suffer, you would try to overcome these
fancies of a sick child. ·You wring my very heart !"

" And you mine !" he stammered. His weak efforts
to push the heavy chair still farther from her made
the old wire padding and casters creak again. " I
beg of you to go," he whispered. " Only go !"

" My darling ! . . . When I have just come to
care for you ! . . . Vladimir, you were never cruel."

"I do not mean to be; . . . that is, I must be
. . . Do you not see my tortures? . . . I wish only
to be alone."

"And can you dream for an instant that, even
although you hated me, I would leave you alone
when I see you ill? See, I will not touch you:
. . . I will only stay as your servant, your nurse.
. . . You cannot refuse that?"

"Just to be alone, . . . to be alone again!" murmured the exhausted man, letting his eyes close
wearily.

"I have said that I will not touch you, Vladimir.
If you wish it, I will not even speak to you. But
you cannot, in humanity, tell me to leave you! You
cannot expect me to obey such a command as that,—
you whom I have cradled on my breast in the most
fearful diseases! Why, I drank your scorching
breath when as a little thing of two you had diph-
theria so that I could get no one to help me nurse
you but a Sister of Charity! When they thought
you threatened with small-pox, it was I—I who
nursed you night and day, who took you into the bed
with me, between the very sheets, and placed your
face upon my bare breast! And you would send me
from you now? Ah, no! no! You are a true man,
tender, gentle, forgiving. You do not really think
of such a thing! My son! . . . my first- and last-
born!"

Nadrovine's eyes were now fixed upon his mother's

crouching form, in an expression of the most agonized
entreaty and suffering. His temples and the hollows
beneath his eyes were beaded with sweat. His breath
escaped draggingly through his half-parted lips, which
moved without uttering a sound. Some one laughed
and ran a halting chromatic scale in the room below
as though trying to make the soulless, rattling in-
strument giggle an accompaniment.

"Little ape! you have been stealing raisins again!"
exclaimed a shrill voice from another direction, and
the sound of two or three smart slaps was followed
by the droning cries of a small child.

"Answer me, Vladimir! . . . Answer me, my
heart, my darling!" urged his mother, still kneeling. Her great fur robes, which the sudden cold
weather had caused her to assume, and which she
had not removed on entering the chilly apartment,
hung in soft splendor about her, and rose into a
muffled background for her face, which shone with
the luminousness of a moonstone in the white light
from the patch of sky above.

"It is too much . . . I have too much . . . " he
stammered, still staring at her.

"Then why do you not wish me to share it?
Why do you send me away? I will do whatever
you wish. See! All is not as you think. All is
not lost. Listen, Vladimir. I will tell you. It is
good news. I will tell you. You shall have her
after all! You shall have her, my own! Vladimir,

speak to me! Speak! . . . Do not sit so rigid. . . . Look at me! . . . Speak to me!" She rose, stumbling over her heavy furs in her eagerness to reach him, but before she could touch him he opened his eyes, and something in their expression arrested her where she stood.

"No! . . . no!" she hastened to assure him, sobbingly. "Do not look at me like that! I am not going to touch you. . . . I swear it!"

The look of relief which crept over his face cut her to the quick. She hurt her hands with their pinching clasp upon each other.

"You shall have her. . . . You shall have her," she repeated, trembling through all her splendid frame.

"Do not speak of her!" cried Nadrovine, in a dreadful voice. He bent upon her another of those looks which had frozen her and with the memory of which she was now trembling.

"I know all,—all. It has come to me in my loneliness and illness as clear as day. Scales have fallen from my eyes. I know everything Everything has been made clear to me. I no longer think that I killed him by accident. No! it was God who drove my sword into the breast of your——" He broke off; his lips remained parted. "No! no! I must not say it! . . . She is my mother; . . after all, she is my mother. . . . "

Madame Nadrovine loosened her great cloak with

a quick gesture and thrust it from her. All of a sudden she seemed suffocating. She stood before him only in her simple black gown, her bosom rising and falling against her clinched hands.

"What is it that you mean?" she said, almost in a whisper.

"Do not act to me, my mother," he replied, sternly. "For in your heart you must believe with me that the man whom I killed I was ordained by God to kill as my father's defender."

His name burst from her in one terrible cry. And then again she uttered it in a heart-broken note of anguish and despair:

"You believe that of me? . . . My God! my God! . . . He believes that I, his mother,—I, his mother,—I, who have worshipped him, who have adored him, yes, adored him before very God, even as Mary adored her Son . . . It is my punishment! . . . It is my punishment! . . . Yes, this is to be my Hell. . . . I will carry it in my breast forever!"

For the first time in his life, Nadrovine saw his mother break into piteous weeping, turning from him and leaning her face on her arms, which she rested against the whitewashed wall. A violent shuddering took possession of him. The Western Railway terminus was not far distant, and the shrill scream of an approaching train mingled discordantly with the chromatic scales which were again sounding from the room below. A girl in the house opposite lighted a great lamp and began to read, rocking back and forth. Nadrovine heard his mother's weeping mingle with the commonplace sounds, in an awful discord. The droop of her dark figure against the white wall was as abandoned, as desolate, as the swaths of crape on white tombstones. Her beautiful dark head was bent almost out of sight under its weight of misery.

"Oh, my God! Oh, my God!" he heard her say over and over again. The young girl in the opposite window, whom he could not avoid seeing from the side of his eye, seemed to be rocking in time to these plaintive, smothered cries. All at once she turned, revealing to him her face marred with anguish,—its loosened, trembling lips, its eyes heavy with tears. She looked all at once her full age. In the cold light from above, her hair seemed suddenly to be streaked with gray.

"Do you know me?" she asked, with faltering eagerness. "Do you know who I am?" It was heart-rending, this last desperate clutching at the possibility of his delirium. "Speak my name. Tell me who I am," she continued, holding herself from him, as it were, with the pressure of her strong hands against her breast.

"Too well. . . . I know too well," he said, in a choked voice.

"But say it, then! say it! . . . Speak my name.

I wish to hear what you will say. I beg it of you !"

"Oh, my mother," exclaimed Nadrovine, "do you not see that you are killing me? . . . I cannot forget. . . . In spite of all,—yes, in spite of all, I love you, . . . God knows !"

He would have gone on, but she flung herself against his knees with a great cry. Her face was radiant, brilliant, tremulous with smiles,—the face of a young mother whose first-born has just been placed in her arms.

"Again,—once more ! Say that you love me, only once again. It is the answer to my prayer. Afterwards the punishment. . . . Vladimir, . . . it is your mother,—it is your mother who humbles herself to you, who prays to you, . . . your small one. . . . I seem to hold you again in my breast. You love me,—you have said it. . . . No matter what you believe of me, you love me."

Nadrovine covered his face with both hands.

"Have pity !" he said, in a hoarse voice.

"But you love me ! . . . you love me ! . . . I can bear anything knowing that. . . . And you will overcome this other horrible fancy. I know it. . . . When you are strong and well again, you will come and kneel to me for forgiveness. Oh, I know,—I !"

She leaped to her feet, straightening her tall figure superbly. "I can bear anything, anything, now," she continued, half chanting the words as she began to move about the little room, drawing a chair into place, fastening back one of the bed-curtains of dim bluish cretonne which had fallen from its loop of tarnished silver cord. She opened the door of the ugly little stove and peeped in to see if it needed replenishing, tossing in a coal or two with her long, white fingers from which she had drawn her gloves. The glowing light fell rosily on her sparkling face, and on the patches of whitewash which remained upon the bosom and sleeves of her black gown from their contact with the wall.

"We must have lights," she said, excitedly. "It is growing dark. And there must be medicine for you to take. Where is it? And when did you lunch? It must be six o'clock. You must have some food. What does the doctor allow you? I will go and fetch it myself."

Nadrovine, weakened, made incapable of any sustained effort, by a wasting illness, seemed suddenly to have yielded.

"You will find the medicine in that little cupboard in the corner," he replied. "Two teaspoonfuls in a wineglass of water."

"And the food, great one,—what must I prepare for you?"

"Nothing. .... A glass of milk at seven, with a little lime-water in it. But I am convalescent now. The medicine is only a tonic."

She poured it out, holding it up between her eyes

and the waning light in order to assure herself of a correct measurement. She then lighted a student's-lamp which she discovered on a small table near the bed, tearing out the fly-leaf of a book to make a lamp-lighter.

"Just a moment," she said, as she placed it near him, "while I bid the *concierge* to send up a boy with my travelling-case."

She was only absent a few moments. From the case, which had been placed on the bed, she took out one of her favorite white crape peignoirs and some pretty, gold-colored *mules*. Her favorite perfume of white lilacs made spring seem an invisible presence in the low, stuffy room. She cast aside her black gown, and assumed the peignoir, stooping herself to unbutton her boots, and with her usual daintiness drawing on stockings of gold-colored silk, in place of the black ones which she wore, before assuming the graceful slippers. She then unfastened, brushed, and re-braided her long hair, humming to herself before the little wavy glass over its shelf in the wall as she did so, with her mouth full of hairpins.

XX.

As she turned from this task, she saw that Nadrovine had apparently fallen asleep. She stood looking down at him, her hand raised half warningly, as though entreating his guardian angel not to rustle her wings too loudly. She did not touch him; she scarcely dared to breathe. It took her some moments to move to the door softly enough and to open it in search of the milk and lime-water which was to constitute his dinner. Having slipped on her boots again and covered herself from head to foot with the fur cloak, she came back with it in a little case for ice which she had gone to purchase herself, and with the last bit of ice which she could find at the nearest chemist's. She placed these treasures in the corner of the room which was farthest from the stove, and then, glancing at Nadrovine, established herself in one of the two remaining chairs, with her feet on the other. It was so still in this lonely street that the hum of the distant thoroughfares reached one no more distinctly than the confused murmur of a shell placed at one's ear, and he could hear plainly the ticking of the little watch which she always wore on her left arm, and which seemed to mark time for the crooning noise emitted by the pan of water on the stove near by.

Nadrovine watched her beneath his half-closed lids for at least an hour before altering his position. He then sighed heavily, and she was at his side in a moment with the glass of milk.

"I am afraid you have gone without it too long," she said, anxiously; "but I could not bear to wake you." He drank it obediently, and she then left him, saying that while he prepared for bed she would sit on the stairway just outside. When she returned he was in bed, and seemed to have fallen asleep again from sheer weakness. She ran her strong hand once or twice down the bedclothes with a gesture of inexpressible tenderness, and then kneeled down suddenly, resting her head and hands against his feet. Her prayer lasted so long that one might have fancied her to have fallen asleep after the excitement of the past hours; but she rose at last, vigorous and self-contained as ever, this time placing herself in the chair which Nadrovine had occupied, and turning down the lamp. The night passed on. Hour after hour slid dayward in a silence broken only by the occasional rumbling jolts of some cart in the street below, and the incessant purring noise of the pan of water, which from time to time she rose to replenish.

A sudden, sharp, clicking sound roused her with a start. Broad daylight drenched the misty air without, and gave to the bleak whitewashed walls surrounding her all the ghastly candor of a corpse's face unveiled by day. Nadrovine was standing, entirely dressed, by the open door. It was the click of the unoiled latch which had awakened her. She was beside him in an instant.

" What is it? . . . What do you wish? . . . Where are you going? I will get anything that you wish. . . . Come! Come back to bed."

Again she thought him delirious, but he answered her gravely and collectedly :

"I had hoped that you would not wake. . . . I must go. I have my senses perfectly. . . . I have thought of it all night."

"Where? Where is it that you are going?"

"To Alceron."

"To Alceron! To Normandy! Whom do you know in Normandy? We have no friends there, —no one to whose house you could go as an ill man."

"I have said that I am convalescent. And then my friend is a priest,—or rather a monk."

"But why do you go to-day? . . . Why were you stealing away from me? Ah! come back, I implore you,—or at least close the door. That chill draught is dreadful."

"I have no time. I must go at once. It is a matter of importance."

"A matter of importance? What can be so important as your health?"

"I must go, and at once."

"You are determined?"

"Absolutely."

"Will nothing,—nothing——"

"No, no. It is imperative. There is nothing to which I could listen."

She stood watching him, her face sharp with anxiety.

"Then I must go with you!" she broke in, interrupting him.

"Impossible!" said Nadrovine, hastily. "I have

only a few moments. It may be that I will miss the train now. There! There is a whistle now."

"That is a train coming in. Cannot you tell the difference? A moment,—just a moment."

"No, I cannot wait. It would take too long. You could not get ready in time."

"But I am ready now," said his mother.

While they were speaking, she had thrust her feet into her boots, and assumed her long fur cloak, which completely hid the white crape gown underneath, and now pressed through the door at his side, fastening on her hat with trembling fingers.

"Come, then!" said Nadrovine, growing paler than ever. She followed him down the long flights of stairs, her unbuttoned boots sounding clumsily on the uncarpeted wood, her hands still nervously busy with her hat. They passed together out into the raw morning air, which was gradually becoming broken and lively with the clattering of the milk-maids' pails, the running of children's feet along the pavement, the bells of hurrying asses, the sound of brooms in the opening shop-doors and laughter issuing from their dim recesses. Before one of these shops a little thing of six was watering the side-walk with a large watering-pot, and some of the spray dashed Madame Nadrovine's ankles as she passed by, her boots still flapping untidily with her swift movements. So unwonted a sight were slovenly feet even in summer Paris that the little *gamine* with the watering-pot paused in her occupation to stare after the tall lady who wore yellow silk stockings in the street and who left her boots unfastened. Even the fruit-venders yawning over their stalls and with their chins and throats gilded by the reflected light from the piles of oranges beneath were transfixed with a sense of bewilderment.

As they rolled out of the great station, the ball of the sun appeared in sodden crimson behind a bank of dense gray, making the soaked, dark masses of the bridges appear more imposing and sombre than ever by its lurid flaring in the water below.

The whole journey was passed in utter silence.

She was at last convinced that the excitement of fever had nothing to do with his actions. He was pursuing some plan long meditated upon, and which her presence had probably brought to a crisis. There were only two other people in the carriage,—an old man, and a child of about nine,—a graceful elf, not unlike little Lotta Boutry with her dark curls and large gray eyes. She amused herself by making a "mouse" out of her small pocket-handkerchief and causing it to jump to different parts of the carriage. By accident it chanced to strike Nadrovine on the hand. He started and turned his head.

"Oh, monsieur! I ask you a thousand pardons!" cried the little witch, growing crimson in a genuine embarrassment. Her likeness to Lotta struck him at once. He smiled.

"Do not look so alarmed, my dear," he said, kindly. "Come here, and I will show you how to make a curé with your handkerchief." And, as the child sidled up to him, he gravely drew a knot in the bit of cambric, and, placing it over his forefinger to represent the curé's head, proceeded to wave his thumb and second finger, as though making the curé gesticulate violently with his arms. He seemed to himself to have suddenly become childish, so easily was he moved to joining in the child's merriment at the antics of this strange little priest. He then talked to her, and told her stories until she fell asleep with her head almost in the pocket of his coat. She and the old man were both asleep when they reached Alceron, and he stooped and kissed her before he got out. Had he glanced at his mother, her drawn, set face would assuredly have struck to his heart; but he did not turn his head in her direction. In fact, he had almost forgotten her presence. His thoughts and sensations seemed to him as unfamiliar as the scenes which surrounded him.

As they walked along the principal street of the little village, they saw that the sun had disappeared, and that a drizzling rain was beginning to fall. The booming of the heavy surf thundered through the damp air, seeming to make the ground vibrate beneath their feet. Far out at sea fell a leaden gleam from a ragged gap in the clouds. The quaint houses of black flint mottled with patches of whitewash seemed pushing against each other in their march seaward. One could see the splendid, yellow-white waves shaking their crests angrily as they reared and plunged against the great stone quay. A sail passed into the glary light far away, tossed wildly for a moment or two, and then dashed on into the gloom beyond, while a keen wind, stinging with salt, swept the street from end to end.

Nadrovine walked rapidly, bending his head to prevent the wind from carrying away his hat, and his mother kept close behind him. Moisture dripped from her hat, from the sables that enveloped her, from her falling hair. Her feet were now drenched, and the constant slipping of the unbuttoned boots had chafed her heels until each step was a pain.

They paused before a small house shrinking back under its projecting roof like a shy child under its hood. Some one spoke through the closed door, and Nadrovine answered in Latin. He was admitted at once, and his mother, shivering under her heavy cloak, crouched down under the shelter of the old portico to wait for him. He returned after an interval of perhaps an hour. A man was with him, a monk, whose heavy cowl pulled forward concealed all of his face except a pale, handsome mouth, and a fine chin, bluish with much shaving.

They passed Madame Nadrovine in silence, and walked together down the slanting street, the monk's heavy gown beating about his limbs in the fresh 'blasts of wind. She struggled after them. Her feet now pained her so intensely that she took off her boots and hid them under her cloak, experiencing a delightful sensation of relief each time that her feet sunk to her ankles in the oozing sand.

The monastery of Alceron is built upon a neck of land that juts out into the sea, and its cliffs are worn away by the boiling waves like a stack of hay nibbled by cattle in winter. It is a great building of dark granite, and utterly out of keeping with the chapels which flank it, and which are specimens of the most soaring Gothic, their slender spires and steeples seeming to pierce the low-hanging clouds with a species of exultation.

Up a narrow stairway cut in the stone, and shiny with moss, Madame Nadrovine followed the two men. She was dazed, breathless, almost callous with mental and physical pain. Her eyes seemed pierced by two red-hot knitting-needles which, ever turning, were thrust deep into her brain. The ceaseless boom of the vast breakers seemed part of the tumult in her hot head.

Unfastening her hat, she let it escape from her hand and fall whirling down into the sea. It skimmed, slanting and dipping, for two or three seconds over the white surge, like a raven with a broken wing, and then disappeared. She pushed back her saturated hair and struggled on. Below stretched the village, the corn-lands, the plunging ocean. A train

rushed through the sodden valley, leaving behind it
volumes of black smoke, which, uncurling lazily,
hung low over the drenched fields until they dis-
solved into the thick air.

As Nadrovine was about to pass within the iron-
bound doors of the monastery, however, his mother
sprang forward and thrust herself between the monk
and her son.

"Tell me, . . . " she cried,—"tell me what it is
that you are going to do !"

The monk stared at her in surprise, drawing away
his gown from the contamination of a woman's garments.

"You shall tell me," she repeated,—"one of you.
Speak !"

"Who is this woman?" said the monk to Nadrovine, and was answered in a whisper, and in two
words :

"My mother."

"Her place is not here," said the monk, coldly.
"Have you not made your farewells ?"

"What is this?   What do you mean ?" cried Madame Nadrovine, fiercely.   "I know nothing !   What
farewells?   My son has been desperately ill with
brain-fever.   He is now out of his mind.   Yes, it
is my belief that he is now a maniac from fever.
What advantage are you trying to take of him?
Vladimir, come; let us return.   This exposure may
mean death to you."

"It is impossible," he said, in a dull tone. He had not once lifted his eyes from the ground.

"You are mad!" said his mother. "You are beside yourself with fever.—You, whoever you are, are taking advantage of an insane man."

"I have been his confessor for eight months," replied the monk. "This step has been long meditated."

"What step? . . . What step?" she exclaimed, angrily. "Vladimir, answer me yourself. I command you."

"Answer, my son," said the monk, in a low voice. And then these words escaped the lips of Nadrovine as though uttered by a machine:

"It is my desire of my own free will to enter the monastery of Alceron as a permanent member, to take the vow of silence, and to live a life of self-denial both in body and in soul."

XXI.

Madame Nadrovine's next action astounded the monk, who expected a violent scene, accompanied by tears and reproaches. She stepped back, gathering her wet clothes about her with one of those royal gestures which she knew how to assume without becoming theatrical, and said, in a clear, self-contained voice,—

"Go, then!"

Nadrovine did not stir. His face preserved its

immobile pallor. Not a muscle started or quivered.

"Go, then !" repeated his mother, in her ringing tones. "Since it is your desire, it is mine also. I wish no love nor duty that does not come to me as a free gift."

The deep notes of the vesper-bell mingled with the strident shriek of a little tug which was approaching the quay below. From the doors of the monastery came a band of monks, solemn, implacable figures in their dark gowns and cowls. They passed by the strange group without appearing to notice it, and entered the chapel to the right. One heard their sonorous chanting muffled by the great walls.

The monk touched Nadrovine on the shoulder. "It wants but an hour of the time, my son," he said.

Madame Nadrovine had not yet relaxed her defiant, towering pose.

As though impelled by some force within, Nadrovine turned and entered the chapel with the monk. The ponderous doors closed behind them. And at that irrevocable sight the whole force and meaning of it all seemed to sweep over the woman like a whirlwind. Dashing herself forward, she beat the doors with her hands, bruising them on the enormous iron nails with which they were studded, weeping, crying aloud, now praying to God, now cursing His cruelty which had taken from her the one creature whom she had ever loved. She looked like a magnificent evil spirit demanding entrance to the sacred place, that she might wreak her vengeance on some hated one within. Her face, dark and swollen with rage, lost every trace of its rare beauty. She called down every ill of earth and purgatory upon those who had enticed her son from her. The savage in her seemed suddenly to have broken through every restraint of tradition and custom, and to have transformed her into a fury whose tongue uttered alternately the most withering blasphemies and cries for mercy like those of an animal which is being vivisected.

Her fury exhausted itself at last, and she sank down on the chapel steps, letting her head lean back against the lintel. Twilight was gathering. A broad, violet-colored star throbbed in the sky between tatters of wind-torn cloud. In the village, and along the quay, lights sprang out against the darkness, and on the little tugs they also twinkled gayly. The monastery was a sullen, uncompromising squareness against the pearl-colored sky. Hoarse screaming and puffings ascended from the water below, sounds of shouting, of bells, of men's and women's voices mingled in drunken laughter. That serene violet flame burned quietly over all. The woman fixed on it her hot eyes. It rested her to imagine it merely an opening in heaven's floor, rather than another world, vast, and with a misery vaster in proportion than this world upon which the wretched drama of her life was being played. The intoning of the monks within reached her in a melancholy cadence, as indistinct, as weird, as the voices of the Seven Sleepers talking in their dreams might have sounded to a listener at the mouth of their cave. She even caught a whiff of the burning incense. Her feet began to ache intolerably, with a throbbing, burning pulsation, and she held them, first one and then the other, in the palms of her hands, which she first cooled upon the stones of the damp wall.

She sat there, it seemed to her, for many hours. The heavy doors opened at last, and the warm air within rushed out, enveloping her in its steam of breath and incense, and the odor of woollen gowns, sandal-wood, leather, moth-eaten embroideries. The monks each carried a tall taper which left behind it a little stream of brown smoke, and which brought out clearly the modelling of mouths and chins. She let them pass, thirty, forty, even fifty, and then she leaped forward and threw her strong arms around the fifty-first. He staggered, swayed, his candle falling from his hand and singeing her hair as it fell. The darkness hid his face. There was confusion among the monks: they wavered and halted, not knowing what had happened.

"Vladimir! Vladimir!" groaned a woman's voice, in an ecstasy of pain,—"my great one,—my

only one,—my son,—speak! Say some word to me!
My son! My son!"

He struggled with her in silence. The solemn
vows which he had just taken sealed his lips. The
other monks were also of a necessity silent. They
jostled against each other in awed curiosity, dropping the hot wax from their tapers on their sandalled
feet and blowing gowns. Many of the candles
were extinguished. One of the monks took Nadrovine by the arm and tried to force him along,
but the woman was stronger than he had thought;
her arms held the knees of her son as in a hoop of
steel :

"Speak to me! Speak to me! I command you,
—I, your mother,—I who gave you birth. You are
my flesh, torn from me with horrible pain. My life,
my youth, everything I have given to you. You
have no right! God will curse you, and all these
with you! You will die horribly! My curse will
be upon you! My curse will be upon all these who
have taken you from me! May God——"

Some one thrust her roughly backward, and she
fell, her head striking one of the stone steps. The
procession passed on. One of the monks hesitated,
and half turned, but was pressed forward by those
behind. They were all received into the vast hall
of the monastery of Alceron, and its vine-wood doors
closed behind them.

When she opened her eyes at last, that violet-hued

star still pulsed quietly over Alceron, but there were multitudes to keep it company. The sky was sown with them, and they pricked the heaving water below with sharp little blades of light.

The noise of laughter and singing still rose from the quay below. On her left the black pile of the monastery wore a solemn grandeur. She lifted her arms towards it and cursed it, together with all its inmates, then, turning, groped her way with her delicate bare feet and hands towards the moss-covered stairway in the rock. That feeling of unreality which always attends one in a 'great crisis claimed and overpowered her. She endeavored to descend the slippery stairs, but, after falling once or twice, sat down and worked her way along by the aid of her arms and the pressure of her feet against the stone directly below her. When she finally found herself at the bottom, she did not know which way to go. Fixing her eyes on the brightest light visible, she began to walk towards it.

After perhaps half an hour, she found herself before a tavern, which was brilliantly lighted for so small a village, with several large oil lamps, but, strange to say, the crowd had collected outside of the open door instead of within.

One of the men caught sight of her as she came forward, her dark hair hanging about her face in sodden disorder, some blood from a wound which she had received in one of her falls when attempting to descend the stone stairway staining her temple and cheek, her robe of sable pulpy and forlorn like the coat of some drenched wild beast.

"You're a pretty sight!" called one of the men, roughly,—a brawny sailor with a head of matted black curls and the jaw of an Irishman. "I say," he roared to the others, "she looks like a bear that has just swallowed a woman all but her head!"

There was a chorus of appreciative laughter. The woman whom they ridiculed stared at them coldly. When the laughter had subsided, she asked, in a calm voice,—

"Why do you stay out here in the street to bellow, when you might be in that room there?"

The crowd received this remark in silence, being rather overwhelmed at her coolness.

"You are one to ask questions, *ma foi!*" exclaimed one of the women, finally, with a light impertinence. "I should wish to know where you would find yourself if we asked you all the questions that we felt disposed to ask!"

"I should remain where I now am and endeavor to answer them civilly," replied Madame Nadrovine, in the same tranquil voice. A little mumbling of applause was heard at this, and she took advantage of it to repeat her question. The people were beginning to see that she was no common character, and one of the men answered her with a certain respect,—

p

" It is Jean Givelot, who is ill with the fever,—
at least with that and a mixture of the drink-crazi-
ness. We were all in there when he was taken. I
went for the doctor. It was droll to see us when
he said what it was. We all tumbled on each other
in our haste to get outside, like so many sheep. Cré !
our sweethearts had to take care of themselves, I tell
you. The devil might have had the hindmost, for
all we cared !" And again a shout of merriment
ascended. As it died away, there could be heard the
groans and entreaties of the man within :

" Do you not see them ? Do you not see them ?
A hundred thousand great pink rats. They are clear
like jelly; one can see through them. And their
tails wriggle like serpents. They nibble me. Oh !
oh ! they are serpents ! They nibble me and sting
me all at once. Oh !"

" You hear," said the man, significantly. " It is
this way with him once every two or three years,
and it is bad enough, God knows; but now that
he has the fever with it, one can't tell where it will
end."

" Who is with him ?" said Madame Nadrovine.

" No one. The doctor has gone to fetch some
one ; that is, if he can find any one just for the night.
A nurse has been telegraphed for."

" Yes, I took the telegraph. The doctor promised
me two sous," said a little monkey who stood by,
expanding his naked brown chest.

."And there is no one with him?" said Madame Nadrovine again.

"No one! not a soul! not even a cat!" resounded from all sides.

She moved forward, pushing open the door, which swung easily at her touch.

"You are all cowards,—all human beings," she said, in her clear voice, and, before they knew it, had passed into the room beyond, through the door with its transparent glass panes which had "Le Café Doré, Jean Givelot Propriéteur," in an arch of gilt letters across its clear expanse. They flattened their faces against the panes, watching her walk across the floor and disappear within a room beyond, from whence issued those dreadful cries.

When the reckless woman entered this apartment she fully expected the crazed man to fly at her and perhaps to strangle her; but he was crouching piteously in a distant corner behind a barricade of chairs and other small articles of furniture, over which his wild face peered timidly, convulsed with fear. He was a small creature, with a lean brown face, hair of that pale hue which seems only a darker shade of flesh-color, and small black eyes under thick, reddish lids. His flaccid mouth worked from side to side over his projecting teeth.

"The rats! the rats!" he moaned. "Oh, help me to drive them away! Each has a little one with it. They are talking rats. They say, 'Jean Givelot,

Satan has sent us to gnaw your heart and let out the good brandy in it!' Yes! yes! I know it. I have known it a long while. My heart is full of brandy, like one of those chocolate bon-bons which Marie sent from Paris last Easter. Oh, the little cold feet! They patter all over me! They leave blisters full of brandy. Oh! oh! I sweat it at every pore. I will melt and stream away under the door, and then those vagabonds outside will dip me up in a cup and drink me! Ah! ah! how I will burn them! I am poisonous through and through. These rats that nibble me,—see how they are dying. There are three layers on the floor. They swell like drums as soon as their teeth go in me. By and by they will be up to my knees, then to my breast. Oh! help! help! They will rise above my head and suffocate me! I shall die horribly! It is what Marie said. She would say, ' Jean Givelot, if you do not mend your ways, some day you will perish horribly.' Oh! oh! Marie! Marie! bonne maman! call away the rats! call away the rats! I will be good! I will be good!"

XXII.

Madame Nadrovine threw aside her heavy cloak, and advanced towards him. He had not noticed her when she entered the room, but now as she approached him in her long white peignoir he uttered a low wail of terror and clutched his face

in both hands, flattening himself against the wall
behind.

"Oh! oh! I called bonne maman! and there she
is in her long white grave-clothes. Good bonne
maman, dear, kind, good bonne maman, don't hurt
your poor, poor little Jean, who promises to be good.
I will never steal the liqueur of the brandied peaches
again. I will take out the stones for you and peel
them all day long. Ugh! how she smells of the
grave! how she smells of the grave!" he ended, in
a lower tone, as though to himself.

"Come," said Madame Nadrovine, soothingly,
"I am not angry. I have come to help you to be
good. See, first I will drive all the rats away." She
took up a towel from one of the chairs and began
whipping the air and floor with it. She walked
slowly around the room, beating it about her, and
then, after making the motions of driving things
out of the door, she closed it and returned quietly.

"You see, they are all gone," she said, in her calm,
reassuring voice, "and I have pushed the dead ones
out with my foot. It is all quiet. Come and lie on
the bed while I say a charm that will make the brandy
in your heart evaporate and let you sleep."

He glanced timidly at her through his quivering
fingers, which he parted a little.

"Then you are not angry? You will not beat
me?"

"Certainly not. You see that I have driven all

20

the rats away.   Come and let me help you on the
bed."

"But, bonne maman, you used always to beat me
when I stole the liqueur; and then, too, you look so
horrible in your long shroud.   It makes me creep
all over.   I feel as though I were lined with ice."

"Silly fellow! this is not my shroud.   This is the
robe that I wear as an angel.   If you will come and
lie on the bed, I will let you hold a fold of it, and it
will make you sleep and drive away all evil dreams."

She began to take away the pile of chairs and foot-
stools one by one, talking to him in a low, even
voice all the while.   He would shrink nervously
away as the white fingers came near him, but sub-
mitted docilely, and at last stepped forward and
allowed himself to be guided to the bed.   Just as
he put one knee on it, however, he gave a howl of
terror and caught Madame Nadrovine about the
knees, plunging his head into the damp folds of
her gown.

"Oh! oh!" he moaned, "there are worms in it!
—black worms, with heads like little goblins,—two
white dots for eyes, and a mark for the nose and
mouth! they are like the figures you used to draw
for me on my slate, bonne maman!   Do not make
me get in there!   I shall die!   I shall die of horror!
They stand on their tails and wave from side to side.
Oh, you will kill me if you make me get in there!"

Madame Nadrovine shook him off with a gesture

of angry disgust. He fell back, supporting himself with one hand, and staring up at her.

"You know you are angry, bonne maman," he whimpered. "You know you mean to beat me. But why did you put the worms there, if you wanted me to get in the bed?"

Great tears began to roll down his face, and he tucked them in his mouth with his tongue as they fell, still blinking up at her. She made a strong effort and regained her patience.

"Come, stupid boy," she said. "There are no worms there now. I have turned them all into little sparrows, and they have flown away. Look, I assure'you it is so."

She finally coaxed him to lie down, and after about fifteen minutes the anodyne which the doctor had given him before leaving began to work, and he fell into a heavy, stertorous sleep, with his flabby lips hanging loosely, and his eyeballs showing in glazed streaks between his fleshy lids.

Madame Nadrovine sat in a low chair opposite the bed, and took in every detail of the unconscious mass of ugliness with her clear, cold eyes,—the thin, clammy hair, streaking the bulging forehead, the puffing in and out of the swollen lips with the harsh breaths that escaped them, the revolting coarseness of throat and nostrils, and the pendulous, red ear-lobes covered with a fuzz of whitish hair.

He slept on and on, and she sat without moving,

never taking her eyes from that bleared face. Her fair, naked feet, covered with dried sand, were crossed unconcernedly in front of her, and she had thrown one of her arms over the back of the chair; the other followed listlessly the curve of her thigh outlined by the damp crape. In the street outside the crowd was thinning, but some remained and whispered together with important noddings and finger-shakings. Every one was on the lookout for the doctor, being desirous to be the first to impart to him the news of the strange woman who had appeared suddenly out of the night, " like a great black witch," as one of the men said.

When poor Givelot's ravings finally ceased, they were more convinced than ever that she had some unholy power which she used freely to soothe him.

"I tell you she is a witch," insisted the sailor, wisely. "She has just the look in her eyes of a Breton woman I once saw, who had eaten the livers of ten black cats, raw, at midnight, lying face down on her father's grave, and after that she could drive out devils and see things that she couldn't feel. I tell you I know what I say!"

Madame Nadrovine continued her silent watch. It had lasted now for nearly two hours. As the clock over the door gave a wheezy click preparatory to striking, she rose and approached the bed. Givelot had not moved. An idea had been forming in the woman's mind for some time past. She put her hand on the pillow, and looked over her shoulder around the room. No one was there. The door was closed and latched. There was a little plaster-cast figure of the Virgin on a bracket at the foot of the bed, and she went and kneeled down before it in silence, her large eyes fastened on its sugar-like pink draperies. Then she rose and came back to the man's side.

"It will be the expiation; it will wipe out that other kiss, and my son will be restored to me."

Stooping, she pressed her fresh, cool lips to those of Jean Givelot, through which his breath, scorching with fever and liquor, escaped in gusts.

It was her desire to woo death in the most horrible way possible, to take the fever, and to be forgiven by Nadrovine on her death-bed.

Before daybreak Madame Nadrovine was herself raving in another room at the Café Doré, but not with "the fever." She was threatened with pneumonia, and the little thermometer which the doctor slipped under her arm already registered one hundred and four degrees.

Nadrovine—or Brother Félicien, as he was now called—having obtained permission from the abbé to have inquiries made in Alceron regarding his mother, she was moved as soon as possible to a home conducted by some Sœurs Blancs about fifteen miles from the village. The journey, though attended with every possible precaution, had the effect of

20*

throwing her again into a hot fever and delirium, in which state she remained for nearly thirteen days. One would scarcely have known her. Her beautiful tresses cut close to her head disclosed its delicate symmetry, which had been somewhat concealed by the abundance of dark braids. Her fine skin had assumed the livid, damp appearance of a wax figure slightly melted by a series of long summer days. Against it her graceful sweeping brows stood out boldly, almost harshly, as though one had tied a narrow band of black velvet about her forehead. Her dark eyes, constantly rolling, could be seen in bluish, raised shadows under her lids. Her cheeks and lips had fallen, becoming drawn and yellowish, and her whole face had that withered look which one sees in a tea-rose that has been placed too near a fire.

Those calm and stately maidens with their serene faces framed in sleek, iron-glazed linen, heard strange words during that month of steady nursing. For hours and hours the monotonous murmur would go on, almost as though she were talking in her sleep. One strange peculiarity was that she rarely unclosed her eyes, and never when delirious. They seemed to be turned inward on her own perplexed, suffering spirit. She always fancied that her son was again a baby lying in her eager arms.

"You see how strong he is," she would say. "When he stretches, his little back is like steel;

and I can scarcely hold his chin when he yawns. And he pinches my breast with his little fingers when he is nursing, until it hurts; I tell you, it really hurts. There are little blue marks where he has hurt me. Oh, it is divine to feel the little mouth drawing my life into his! It seems as though I were full of the light of heaven, and that he fed upon it instead of milk. I did not wish a child, you know. Now I do not wish anything else. He lies in my breast at night until the warmth of his little body makes us both moist where our flesh comes in contact. Sometimes I love him so that I desire to hurt him. Then I have to call to Elsa to come quick! quick! I tell her, and she laughs. She tells me that I will not feel so when I have six more just like him. Just like him! The blessed Mary knew that no other could be like her first-born; and it is so that I feel. 'Out of the strong came forth sweetness.' It is like that about Ivan and his son. All the love that I ought to have given my husband I give to his child. That is not disloyal. It is part of him as well as of me. I love him in loving his son. Oh, I cannot bear to think that my baby's lips will ever be pressed to those of another woman with more love than they have felt for me! I do not wish him to marry. Perhaps he will be a great priest. Oh, I cannot let him grow out of my arms into those of another woman! Just to think that she who may steal him from me is perhaps yet unborn, that perhaps they who are to be her parents are yet unknown to each other! May they never meet! I wish that in heaven I may always rest without pain, as one after great pain, with my baby in my arms. I do not wish another. It would seem like sacrilege. Perhaps the Virgin Mother would let me whisper to her of my bliss. Perhaps she would come sometimes and talk to me while I nursed him, and kiss his beautiful brow. And I would tell her of how I feared and dreaded, and perhaps she would tell me that she had feared and dreaded too. And then we would both fall to sleep upon her breast. Oh, he is so sweet!—so sweet! Look at his little chest: Elsa says that it is very broad, the broadest she ever saw. He will be tall, and very strong. Oh, to think that the day will come when he will be stronger than I am! Ah! if we could only die together now and remain a mother and child forever in heaven!"   .

It was in this way that she would murmur on for days and nights at a time.

XXIII.

It was only two weeks after Nadrovine had taken his vow, and at the height of his mother's illness, that he was sent on an errand of mercy to a family of starving wretches who were also ill with the fever, and who lived in Vaudebec, a village some ten miles distant. The road lay inland for about seven miles, and then followed the coast, which was totally unlike the rocky cliffs upon which Alccron descended in a series of terraces towards the quays. The beach was a broad, level stretch of fawn-colored sand, across which the figure of a girl rolling her wheelbarrow of sea-weed would come out into picturesque relief as she walked slowly, her sabots compressing the wet sand about them until it looked like cracking ice with each footstep. Now a woman on a donkey approached, her figure reflected, broken but life-like, in the strips of sand-divided pools in front. Children rolled laughing in the hazy sunlight, adorning themselves with shells and broad ribbons of sea-weed, and burying one another in the sand. One little imp of seven snatched away his sister's neckerchief as Nadrovine advanced, leaving her plump, reddening shoulders bare, in order to pull it over his charmingly impertinent little visage, as though it were a cowl. He held his hands folded and walked along behind Brother Félicien, imitating to the full compass of his sturdy legs the monk's slow, swinging gait. Nadrovine turned and smiled at him over his shoulder. The pranks of children never irritated him.

He reached the village at last, and was returning saddened and inexpressibly exhausted by the brutal, violent misery which he had witnessed, when a clear voice roused him,—a child's voice.

"Oh!" it rang out in a note of distress, " what

shall I do? My poor Zi-Zi! I buried him alive just to have an effect on that hard-hearted Nicoletta, and now I can't find his grave!"

Nadrovine stopped short, not knowing which way to turn, and little Lotta Boutry flashed by him on her slender red-silk legs, her frock of white flannel blowing back in the steady wind, and her dark head uncovered. The child's skirts touched him as she flew. And then another figure advanced. It was Ilva, so slight, so pale, that she looked like a moonbeam which had assumed a woman's shape. She wore a gown of black serge, and there was a black silk handkerchief knotted about her throat. She had no hat, and carried a large raw-silk umbrella over her shoulder, turning it listlessly as she walked. One could see the violet tones of delicate health in her throat and temples at some distance.

She smiled in answer to the child's appeal, but her eyes were piteously grave in contrast. Her voice was so low that Nadrovine could not hear what she said; he only saw that they were coming towards him hand in hand. His presence of mind forsook him utterly. He had that sensation of being petrified which assails one sometimes in a dream where one finds one's self standing on a railway, facing an advancing train, and yet powerless to leap aside. They were quite close to him; the child almost touched him. A fatal weakness came over him, a deadly sensation of blackness, in which the world seemed swing-

ing in great circles, and his very marrow dissolving
in an icy nausea.

"Oh, cousine!" shrieked the child, "look at the
poor monk! He is ill! He is falling!"

He felt the girl's nervous arm thrust under his, and
her slight figure brace itself to support him.

"Lean on me, I beg of you," she said, anxiously.
"You must be suffering very much. Are—are you
hungry?" she stammered a little with a gracious
embarrassment. "We have our luncheon here,
which we do not want. We were just talking of
giving it to the first little child that we met. I
pray you to lean on me. I am much stronger than
I look." He was forced to catch at the delicate
shoulder in order to stand. Her eyes fell on his
bare hand. It was sufficient.

"Vladimir!" she said, in a voice which seemed
to sweep away earth and sky and to leave only their
two lives beating there against each other once more.
It was only an instant: in another he had freed himself of her touch and stepped back, shuddering violently, and trying to conceal his face from her. She
followed him; she held him again with her hands.
Again all things seemed to slip from him, but the
consciousness that she was there, near him, and that
her voice spoke his name. He could not even say
hers in return. His lips were sealed. His newly-
taken vows bound him. All his blood seemed foam-
ing upward to his heart and swelling for a vent.

He tried to shake her off. She held him desperately: they half slipped, and in recovering himself his cowl was shaken back.

"Oh, my God!" she cried, in a tone of indescribable pain, "will you not even speak to me? And you have been ill. You are changed. You look older. It frightens me! You frighten me! Run, run, Lotta,—run away to your dolls. I will come presently. I have much to say to Signor Nadrovine."

The child went at once, her little, serious face pallid with the excessive greatness of the shock. She could not resist turning her head every now and then, as she walked away, to see what they were doing. They still stood where she had left them, Nadrovine with his head bent and turned away, Ilva with her whole figure yearning towards him, her hands locked together in a gesture of impassioned prayer. The child sat down in the shade of the umbrella which she rested on the sand, and tried to compose herself by talking to her dolls.

"I was going to get maman to make you a monk's gown, my dear Zi-Zi," she said, gravely; "but I don't think it will do. It seems to change people horribly. I don't think I should ever have known Monsieur Nadrovine if it hadn't been for Cousine Ilva. Perhaps when Viola gets broken—yes, perhaps then I will let you have a monk's gown." She had placed the umbrella, with her usual dainty discreetness, so that it hid Nadrovine and Ilva from her sight, and she was so far away that she could hear nothing.

"I know you will speak to me, I know you will speak to me, Vladimir," the girl was saying. "What is it? Are you too ill to speak? Oh, Vladimir, tell me what to do. Think of what I have suffered. I would have died, I think, only I was so strong I could not. I used to think sometimes, 'Now it is coming. This pain is too awful to last. God would not wish one to endure such pain any longer.' But then a dulness would come for a time instead of death, and I would feel nothing for hours. I could not even believe that I had ever felt anything. It did not seem to me as though I could have suffered as I thought. And then, all at once, when I felt safe and was trying to think only of heaven and the peace of God, it would come crashing back. I used to feel as though my soul and body were being ground together in a great red-hot iron hand. Oh, Vladimir, you are mine,—you are my very own, as I am yours! You promised —you vowed it to me. Any vows that you have taken since cannot wipe out those. Oh, Vladimir, remember! You have been ill. It was a madness. I know it so well. Many and many a time I have longed to become a nun, and then I would think, 'No! God means us to meet again. He means us to have each other. I feel it. I must wait. I must

L q   21

be patient.' Vladimir, I have been so patient,—I
have waited so long—— My God! he turns from
me! . . . He does not love me any more! He does
not love me any more!"

A groaning cry was wrenched from Nadrovine.
In a moment the girl was on her knees beside him,
kissing his coarse gown, reaching upward with her
little, thin hands for his, clutching his wide sleeves,
sobbing, laughing, talking, all in a breath :

"Vladimir, Vladimir, you will speak to me?
You do love me? You will tell me everything,
my darling, my darling? Oh, was it because you
thought my father's death would stand between us?
Vladimir, I prayed to our blessed Lord with fasting, to guide me, and as it was an accident, . . . as
it was an accident—— Oh, Vladimir, at least we
can love each other, if we cannot be married. At
least you will let me love you, and know that you
love me. Dear, I knew that it would come between
us. I knew that you thought I would never forgive
you. You did not know me. You did not know
me. Ah, but the sun can be a witness to my love
for you! Ah, Vladimir, Vladimir, it is such joy to
see you, to be with you again, that it is almost as
much a pain as sorrow. Oh, turn your face to me!
let me see your eyes,—let me see you, Vladimir!
Give me your hands and lift me up."

She kneeled, straining her slight body upward, yet
without touching him, her pure face as pathetic in

contrast with her slender black-gowned figure as a flower left blooming on a charred stem.

He dared not look at her. He tried not to hear her,—not to think.

She waited for him a long while. At last she said, in a voice exquisitely gentle in its faltering grief,—

"Then you do not love me?"

Again she waited. At last she rose from her knees, the damp sand clinging in patches to her black skirt.

"I will go. . . . It must be very painful. If you will pray for me sometimes, . . . I will always . . . I will always . . ." She stopped, struggling to control herself, and putting her hand to her throat, which ached sharply. "I will . . . yes, always . . . it is for always with me . . . I have taken no new vows . . . It cannot be a sin for me . . . But sometimes, . . . if you will, . . . just a word when you pray for—for those who are not happy . . . . Since you will not speak to me, if you will only lift your hand . . . I will understand, . . . and . . . and go."

There was another silence, and then she turned to go, very slowly, dragging each slender foot as though in bodily pain. All at once he turned, straightening his whole figure. He held out his arms to her, his face blanched with an unutterable struggle. His voice rang out calling her name:

"Ilva! . . . Do not go. . . . I am a coward.

. . . But I love you." As she rushed towards him,
lightly, swiftly, her arms extended almost like a thing
flying, his hands dropped at his sides.

"Do not touch me," he said. "I am a coward,
. . . and perjured. Do not let me break more than
one vow. . . . I will speak,—yes; but I must not
touch you. . . . Help me. . . . You see how weak
I am. Do not tempt me!"

"Oh, my dear one," she answered, "indeed, indeed
I will not. I will even go at once, if you wish it.
It is enough to have heard you say that you love
me. Tell me, what is it that you wish of me? Why,
I could take your hand and walk calmly out into the
sea there and be drowned with you if it was needful.
Or I could go by myself, if it would help you. Just
to have seen you and heard you speak, saying you
loved me,—and then my name once more,—ah! that
was sweet!" She stood gazing at him, great tears
brimming in her eyes, and her hands clasped together
against her breast.

"Tell me; and whatever you say, I will do it,"
she repeated.

"Forgive, . . . forgive!" stammered the man,
completely overmastered. "It is terrible to suffer
so. . . Perhaps for me . . . but what have you done,
. . . my star, . . . my lily?" He muttered to himself, "My God, my God! Thou wast crucified. . . .
Have mercy."

"Oh, Vladimir," said the girl, "do not think that

I will give you more to bear! I will try to help you in every way. I am here as long as you need me. And when you bid me to go,—ah, you shall see how obedient I will be."

"It is not as you think," he said. "*That* came between us. Yes; . . . but I did not mean it. There was more. I can never explain; but you will trust me. There was more,—more,—which made it impossible. . . . It was for that I became a monk. But you will believe that I would have been true to you in love and in purity with nothing but your memory to bind me until I died." These last sentences rang out passionately, unbroken, triumphant.

"Oh, with all my soul! with all my soul!" she cried, her face radiant. "I trust you, believe you, love you! It will be forever!"

"Yes, forever," he said, making the sign of the cross between them. They stood gazing at each other in a heart-broken silence.

"And you must go away from me?" she said at last, wistfully. "I must leave you? . . . Tell me," timidly, "would it be a sin for me just to kiss your hand?"

He could not answer her, and, taking his silence for consent, she approached him; but he folded his hands in his sleeves, making a faint gesture of negation with his head.

"I must not?" she said, her sweet face falling. "Well, then, since you wish it. . . . You shall see

21*

how brave I am. . . . Must it be without anything,
. . . without even so much as touching your hair?
. . . Well, then, I will,—I will. . . . I ask the
dear Christ to be with you. . . . Perhaps if I am
patient . . . And there is all eternity. It will be
a sweet pain . . . to wait for you. . . . And I am
not very strong."

Nadrovine buried his face in his hands, trembling
in every limb. The tide was going out. The shallow
pools glowed like vast opals in the level light of the
sun. The west was brilliant with crimson clouds in
the shape of a great flamingo flying southward.
Lotta, tired of her one-sided conversation with her
wax and china family under the umbrella, had taken
off her shoes and stockings and was wading about
among the pools. She was quite far out,—a tiny
splash of indigo among the soft and vivid hues of
heaven and water.

"Ah, don't! don't!" pleaded Ilva. "You break
my heart. . . . And, after all, . . . is it not a sweet
thought? . . . We shall have each other there. . . .
I will be so patient, so brave. . . . Ah, Vladimir,
. . . I have such a beautiful thought, . . . oh, a
thought so divine that my flesh seems to melt away
and leave me just my soul to remember it! It is
this: I will live so pure, so true, so good a life on
earth, that when I come to you in heaven I will
take you by the hand, and you shall hear with me
the words that our dear Lord will say to tell me of

the joy that I have given Him and the love that He
has always poured upon me!"

Nadrovine remained gazing at her in unspeakable
awe and adoration. The whole light of the gorgeous
sky was upon them. Her pale hair was like still
flame about her face,—like a halo. He felt that he
must kneel to her as in worship. And there was a
beautiful, happy smile on her face.

All at once a shrill cry rang out, bringing them
back to earth:

"Cousine! . . . cousine! I am sinking! I am
sinking in a great hole!"

They flew together. The child was already up to
her knees in the quicksand. Wrapping his arms
around her, Nadrovine drew her out by a supreme
effort, and threw her from him as far as he could.

"Run! run!" he called to her. "Ilva, run, my
darling! I do not know how far this slough reaches.
It has me,—I feel it. Run for help!"

She turned from Lotta, whom she had hastened to
soothe, and saw that his heavy weight had caused
him to sink nearly to his waist in this short time.
She knew that help was impossible. Her mind was
made up in an instant.

"Run! run, Lotta!" she said, echoing his words.
"Run for help, and do not look back, or you will
lose time."

The child started off like a hare. With a swift
movement Ilva sprang into the quicksand at Na-

drovine's side.   She put her arms about his neck, her lips to his.   Far along the broad brown sands the light figure of the child scudded with the speed of desperation.   The distant tide made a soft moaning.   A flock of sails leaning to westward passed into a shaft of rose-colored light.   The clouds floated on serenely,—of gauze,—of soft wool,—of banners of crape across the heavens.   At last the sky was a placid dome of topaz above the quiet sea.   Over shore and inland a beautiful peace brooded, broken only by the calm wings of a nestward dove, the one living thing visible.

The Sun had been a Witness.

THE END.

www.ingramcontent.com/pod-product-compliance
Lightning Source LLC
Chambersburg PA
CBHW030815020726
47499CB00006B/1933